B. D. Pedersen

The
Perfect Picture

Edited by

June Pedersen

ISBN: 13: 978-0692320846

Prologue

Normally it doesn't take much for me to get myself into some kind of trouble. But this time I had to work for it and I didn't even know when I first crossed the line.

It was a hobby and that included my two friends. We had been doing this for years and totally enjoyed it. Who would think that our hobby would be the cause of my friend's deaths and cause me to run all the way across the country trying not to be included in that life category, that is death?

I don't mind telling you that I was scared and would have done just about anything to avoid my appointment with it at that time. The other side of the story was the fact that death was looking for me in the form of aliens.

That's right I said aliens. You know those little green men type beings. Except these guys were huge and any one of them could have eaten me for lunch.

Hell, what did we do wrong that would cause these guys to hunt us down and start killing us? It hadn't occurred to me that we had stumbled on to something important. Right then and there I was concerned about what was happening to my buddies and what was coming at me.

All I know is that we had planned this trip for months and when we took it things that were totally out of our control took place. We ended up taking a picture of something we shouldn't have. We didn't know it, but it meant we would have to die and those wanting us dead would pursue me across the whole of this country.

If it wasn't for some mysterious benefactor, I would have gone the way of my buddies. Someone or something was protecting me and now I believe was also leading me away from those who were out to kill me. What I didn't know was it, they, them, or whatever was doing the same for another innocent witness.

Over the course of time we, the other witness and I, would meet and learn to fight this thing together. She would become my closest confidant and most dependable person I could have ever met. Still, they wanted us both dead and the whole of the southwestern United States would experience the wrath of the aliens that were after us.

What none of us knew was that this entire situation was being orchestrated by another, a force so powerful, so deadly that just the thought of his presence would send spasms of fear through the minds of those pursuing me. A being whose only purpose is to track down and eliminate, to the last being, those who were after me and they had little or no defense against his coming and his actions.

I was to witness the truth about this universe we live in, and just how deadly and dangerous it really was. I was to learn that life as we know it can end in a heartbeat and in ways no one even wants to think about.

I would meet the Gilgons and come to know their hate for any other living creature. Their primary purpose is to find other worlds and strip them of all their resources. In doing that they left a dead planet unable to support the life forms that made that planet home.

What was to stand between them and myself and my world was one being, one most powerful and frightening being that even the power of the Gilgons would bow to. This would be the Hunter.

A being whose life was created and designed with one purpose and only one purpose, the total destruction of the Gilgons wherever they may be found across the whole of the Milky Way Galaxy.

He would be a being that I could never even begin to understand, but I would see him in action and feel the impact of his power. I guess you would call it a love and hate relationship. He had little concern for the welfare of mankind, but did care that the Gilgons did not destroy our world.

He would sacrifice tens of thousands of us here on earth, but guarantee total safety to two of us at that same time. All, as a means of teaching the people of earth that there is more to the universe than we ever thought possible, much of it was dangerous to our survival. What else can I say other than having you come along with me as I tell you of my story and its unbelievable happenings?

Chapter One

ON THE RUN

Fruit, I just can't get enough of it. I'm eating the damn stuff day in and day out. I bet I've spent three hundred dollars on fruit alone in the last three weeks and I still can't get enough. It wasn't that way when I was living on the east coast, but after moving out here to the west coast I eat the stuff all the time.

It was not a normal trip in that I slipped out of New York at three in the morning and headed south until I could tie into Interstate 40 and head due west. I didn't stop until I was well out of the main metro areas of the east coast. I'm not saying that I was running from anything, but I'm running and I was getting out for my own good. Things were completely out of control for me to stay any longer. Besides they would have killed me if they had caught me. The fact is that they may actually do it anyway if they ever catch up with me.

This whole mess started out with the three of us doing our own thing and never thinking that it would be something that others would take exception to, especially in the manner and way they took exception to our actions. Look, we did nothing illegal. It was our hobby and we enjoyed doing it, but somehow, we managed to push someone's button and that spelled the end for two of us.

I'm fairly certain that they will follow me once they have determined that I did in fact leave the area. Whether they will be able to track me all the way out to California, I'm not sure, but I figure that I had better take the necessary precautions and finish getting lost and by that, I mean lost forever.

I started my identity change as I left the east coast. Having never done this before I had to take great pains to ensure that I was in fact not leaving a trail that they could pick up.

I had all the cash I needed to start over so there was no need for me using any traceable expense systems such as credit cards or debit cards or whatever. I went total cash and actually destroyed my cards and identification including my license. There had to be no trace of them and so they were burnt and the ashes mixed into the dirt where I had parked. I would be leaving my car at this location and everything else that I owned except for my back pack and the money and weapon I had inside of it. The only thing I couldn't leave or change was my appearance and that would have to wait until I was on the west coast. No, that won't do, it has to be now, right this minute, right here and right now.

I had reached Durham, North Carolina on I-85 where I then got onto I-40 and headed west at Greensboro. I drove all night until I found the truck stop just outside of Black Mountain, North Carolina. I had traveled around seven hundred miles and needed to stop and let myself calm down. I had breathing room now and it was time to plan. It was there that I burned my identification and left my car.

Hunter sat there at the counter eating his breakfast and drinking a cup of coffee. He had seen the man come into the restaurant and take a seat and order breakfast. For all the trouble he was in he appeared to be doing well. Yes, he was scared, but he was thinking as well, so he knew that with a little help he could get the guy to the place he needs to be before this thing really starts to happen.

He had been on this planet for the last three months preparing for his extermination of the Gilgons and the education of this planet concerning hazards from space. Until now he had only seen one other, besides this one, manage to escape capture and death at the hands of the Gilgons. That meant that this person was one of interest to the Gilgon command and he could be used to set them up for the ultimate confrontation.

Hunter really didn't have any feeling for this being. All he was to him was a tool, a target, or bait for the Gilgons and that would make his job that much easier. He did have a degree of respect for him because of his ability to think and avoid the ultimate capture by the Gilgon and subsequent death at their hands. So, in many respects he would survive because of the marking that Hunter was about to give to him.

Yes, he needed to be tagged and once tagged he would be able to track and mark his activities. From then on and when the time came, he would be able to lead the Gilgons to him and in that way, he would set them up for extermination, something this world would never forget and be scarred by for ten thousand years.

Hunter reached out to the man and touched his mind. It was not that complex a mind but it was well developed and surprisingly strong and quick in its workings. Yes, this was the right one and this was the one they, the Gilgons, would expend all and everything to find and remove. He now had two heading for the West Coast. It was time to meet this being.

As I sat there in the restaurant, I noticed a guy sitting at the bar eating his breakfast. He looked over at me and waved me over to him. I got up and walked over to him. "You looking for a job?" He asked.

That kind of caught me by surprise and I automatically nodded. "Why, yes I am. You have a job you need done?"

He was the usual truck driver and I knew that from time to time they would hire locals to help them with a loading or unloading job. He seemed to be on the up and up and he in no way looked like the guys I was running from. He was around five ten and probably weighed in at two hundred. In other words he was a husky guy with the usual truck driver gut on him.

There was a sense of friendliness about his persona and his eyes were easy but attentive. He gave me the impression that he could easily take care of himself and that he feared nothing, and anyone considering being a problem to him had better have second thoughts about it.

He swung around looking at me. "Yes, I have a couple of deliveries here in Black Mountain and then I will be heading west to Ashville where I have about three hours of unloading to do. You got the time for that?"

I couldn't believe my luck. "Yes, I've got the time and yes I need some work." With that we finished our breakfasts and walked out to his truck where I climbed into the shotgun seat and waited.

When he got in the truck and started out to wherever we were going, he started to talk about where he had been coming from and where he was going. "Been a hard day for me, the last two load drop offs resulted in several items being damaged."

He shook his head and continued. "That means that I'll have to retain those items and make up a return to sender form and then take the time to see that those damaged goods in fact get back to the sending party. That's one hell of a pain in the butt and on top of that the receiving parties had let it be known that they needed those items and that they would be holding me responsible for any losses they may suffer."

I had noted that he spoke in a rather correct or measured style, not the usual truck driver jargon or slang. In fact, there was no profanity or other terms that one would normally attribute to this profession, not that there was anything bad about that. Drivers just had their own means of communication and his did not fit. Oh well, it was not that big a deal. I had a ride out of the area and I was going to make a few bucks while I was at it.

Hunter had now taken the opportunity to tag this being and set into motion the final process in which he would bring the Gilgons to their knees and ultimate destruction. The being he had tagged worked out to be the perfect one for his plan. He and his friends had walked head long into a Gilgon execution and not only that, they had taken pictures of the execution.

Hunter had known that something big had happened when he felt the turmoil in the

Gilgon ranks. A serious error had been committed and the command element of their expeditionary forces was just a little upset with those who had been carrying out the execution of the Gilgon traitor. How they could have initiated their actions in such a public place was highly questionable and as a result they would have to follow up and correct their error. If they failed, then that failure would result in additional executions.

Hunter knew by the quick response and actions of the Gilgons that something important was taking place. Their pursuit and killing of two of the beings in the party of three was something really important. He had targeted the third member of that group of friends and he needed to be involved at this time. As he moved into the region, he found the running being and then started his initial analysis of what had taken place. He was pleased with the results and had decided to assist this being in his attempt to elude his pursuers.

He needed this being in California, along with the other one from Florida, and that meant that he would have to run interference for him all the way across this part of this world. That was not a big problem, but it would require direct and close contact with this being. That was when he worked the plan to bring the being in to close contact with him and tag him. It all worked perfect.

We made three deliveries in Black Mountain and then headed on to Ashville. It was almost six o'clock when I finished and he paid me off and I walked away from the depot where he was parked. Funny I never learned his name and he never asked me for mine.

I had never worked with a trucker before and had never done any delivery work. It seemed odd to me that some of the names on those items being delivered were names I had never seen before. The fact was I didn't know if they were individuals or corporations.

The one name that stood out was that of Gaa, what the hell kind of a name was that anyway? Gaa, there was something to that name and I felt that I needed to remember it, that it would become important sometime in the future. Oh well, what the hell anyway.

A plan started to formulate in my mind and I headed for the town library hoping that it would be open when I got there. As it turned out I was only two blocks from the library and it was open. I needed a computer and when I got into the place, I found one free and ready for use. I needed some paper work so that I could get a new license and new identification. That meant that I needed a birth certificate and with that I went into the web and found the form I wanted and printed it out.

I then went back into the web and searched out all the data I needed to fill out the certificate. I needed a location of my birth, a hospital, a doctor, mother and father, and so on and I needed everything to match up so that the hospital could actually be found in the city I picked as well as the doctor. The parents did not need to match that closely.

After about two hours I had the data I needed and then started looking for a typewriter. I thought that it was going to be a hard find, but after looking around in the place I found one off in a corner all by itself. This was working out perfect.

I sat down and filled in the certificate and then went looking for a stamp. I needed something official looking and when I used it, I wanted it to be faded yet readable to a degree. Whoever looked at it had to be able to determine that it was official and that was all it had to be. As it turned out my certificate was from Georgia and I was in North Carolina that would do. All I had to do was produce something that would make me a resident of North Carolina. I found my stamp in a second-hand store less than a block from the library.

There were two priorities at this point. One was a residential address and the other a car. I found a motel room and settled down for the night. The next day I located a furnished apartment in a large complex and managed to lease it under my new name. That was my first priority at that time.

My second was the car, and I set out for a used car lot where I could find a good quality car and hopefully drive it off the lot without a license. I was fortunate in that during these times the economy was not doing too well so the need to sell was high and the desire to satisfy were just as high. With that I was able to find and purchase a car. My new address and birth certificate cleared all the issues that may have been a problem with the car salesman.

I had my new address, my new used car and the birth certificate that I had made. So, I headed for the licensing bureau. There was a gamble here in that some sharp-eyed employee would spot my phony certificate and then I would be faced with trying to explain myself to that person and everyone else in the place.

I had spent the last two days aging the certificate so that it looked used and genuine. I folded it numerous times and put it in my wallet and then pulled it out I don't know how many times. When I was done it looked like it had been around for years and that I had used it a lot.

The Hunter had been monitoring his target being and had worked closely in the development of his plan and in obtaining his residence and the new used car. If this being had known that there was an external influence, he didn't show it. Hunter would still be monitoring him at the licensing office and making sure that everything went as planned. His other target had been moving across the lower region of the country and doing quite well.

When I got to the licensing office, I was asked for my old state license and I had to think of a reason for me not having one and I told him that I didn't have a license. That my last license had been in Canada about a year ago and that I was now making my

20

permanent residence there in Ashville and I gave them my new address. I presented my birth certificate and he looked it over.

The clerk accepted my reason and my certificate and then advised me that I would have to take a written exam and then a driving exam in order to get the license, I agreed to that. I took the exam and passed with flying colors. The clerk looked at the score and then at me and gave me a weak smile and proceeded to finish the paper work.

He then looked at me and asked that I wait a few minutes and he walked away from me. Had he found me out? That I didn't know, but I was in the fire now and I had to stay put and deal with whatever came next.

After several minutes he came back. "You're in luck. We just had a scheduled driving test cancel and the examiner said she would take you if you're up to it at this time."

I looked at him and must have had a bit of shocked look on my face. "Why yes, I would love to get that done and over with, when do I take it?"

He told me to have a seat and my name would be called and I would be able to take the test and finish everything. It crossed my mind that this could be a setup and that they were just trying to keep me there while the police were responding to take me into custody for having a forged birth certificate. It was a waiting game and there was nothing I could do about it.

Maybe twenty minutes later my new name was called, Darrel Gibson, and I missed it the first time. I was sitting there looking at a magazine and the examiner called, Darrel Gibson. That time I caught it and stood up. "Sorry, I was really into that article and did not hear you. How many times did you call me?"

"Just once Mr. Gibson and that's not unusual. Please come with me."

I followed her out the door and she asked where I was parked and I pointed out my new used car. She walked around to the passenger's side and started to open the door but I had failed to unlock it. I finally figured that out and she got in. I looked at her and shrugged my shoulders. She smiled and then started filling out paper work. Twenty minutes later I was pulling back into the parking lot having finished my driving test. I sat there looking out the window trying to be as normal and easy going as I could, but my guts were turning over just waiting for the right sign from her.

Finally, she looked over at me. "Good job Mr. Gibson I have few drivers who pass this driving test with that high a mark. You can go back inside and finish things up. Do you have any questions?"

I answered her that I had no other question and went back into the waiting room. Another fifteen minutes and I was walking out to my car, temporary license in hand.

So, there I was I had a new used car with a North Carolina temporary license in the rear window, and I had a temporary driver's license under my new name Darrel Gibson. It would be another two weeks before my permanent driver's license would arrive at my new address.

I would have to check back in at the car lot to pick up my new license plates in two days. So, everything was set and all I had to do was sit tight and wait. That two weeks would be the most uncomfortable I had ever had. I still needed to get to the west coast and this three-week layover here in Ashville was not helping.

Hunter's job was how to keep Gaa from discovering the two targets. The one witness while he was still in town and the one to the south. It had been a throw of the dice that Peter, that is Darrel, had stopped here in the town of Ashville, the same place that Gaa had his headquarters on this planet.

It was an accident that Darrel had driven himself into the exact center of the Gilgon's base of action and it would be Hunters task to keep that little issue out of the minds and sight of the Gilgons. It made no difference for Darrel. He knew nothing of it anyway.

I was sure there was a tracker behind me and I needed to finish the death of Peter Danials and get the hell out of here. That's right my real name Peter Danials, but for the time being I'll not go into my past and where I came from. Let's just leave that until I get to the west coast.

Chapter Two

THE END OF PETER DANIALS

Three and a half weeks later I was pulling on to Interstate 40 west bound, heading for the west coast. Peter Danials had arrived in Ashville, North Carolina in the shotgun seat of an eighteen-wheeler and disappeared. Peter Danials had been a tall blond-haired, clean-shaven man in his mid-thirties. As he walked away from the truck and its driver that afternoon around six o'clock, he would never be seen again.

The driver in the new used car that had just entered the freeway going west on I-40 was black haired with a dark mustache and beard. His name was Darrel Gibson and he was a man with no history or background. He had been born in Ashville, North Carolina two and a half weeks ago and was now leaving that new found life behind and heading out to something more his style and that fit his needs.

It was during that trip west, as I crossed the Rocky Mountains, that I started a craving for fruit. It was insatiable, I had to have fruit and I had to have it there with me every minute of every day. I had no idea what was going on, all I knew was that I had to have it.

Fruit, what was there about fruit that was causing me to be craving it so badly? When I was growing up and then after I got out on my own until now at age thirty-two, I had not had any particular interest in fruit. Oh, I ate it once in a while, but for the most part if I wanted something to eat, fruit was the last thing I thought about. So, why am I wanting it so badly now?

It always comes down to that last point, why? There was something going on here and I was starting to think that it was tied in to the reason for me running in the first place. I guess it's time that I went into the reason. I need to think this thing through and determine if the two issues are tied one to the other.

It all started with me and my two buddies Ty and Jacob. I had known those two from school. I'm not really sure how far back in school it was when we first started hanging out together. I had known them before that but we had nothing to do with each other. It must have been around the seventh grade when we were around thirteen and fourteen years old. Ty and Jacob had already been running together for some time by then and I happened to fall in with them one day.

We had been involved with a science field trip and ended up on the same discovery team. We hit it off even though we were almost the last to finish our discovery assignment. We had a great time and that was the start of our hanging out together. We stayed close all through high school and after we had graduated.

We even got involved in the construction trade together and ended up doing our apprentice training at the same time. We ended up working different jobs but from time to time would be on the same job location together. But during our off time we were stuck tight to one another.

It was during this time that we started playing with photography and finally found ourselves completely drawn into the techniques and processes of photo taking and editing. There was no plan to go professional in that field, we were making too much money in the construction trade and it was steady and in demand. No, the photography was something that we concentrated on during our weekends.

None of us had any steady girls at the time and we felt that we had all the time in the world to deal with that later. We were having a great time traveling and taking pictures. The problem was that one of those trips would prove to be the start of an experience that you could only classify as terrifying.

Damn, we were just shooting shots on a lake in upper New York State. Our main goal was a series of landscapes that we wanted to then stitch together in to a panoramic scene. In those days you had to set the camera at the proper position and maintain the focus of each shot as you redirected the camera for each photo in the series.

We had searched for two days for the exact spot to set up and make the shoot. We did not care if there were people in the shots or not, the point was to capture real life activities.

It was while we were doing that, something took place across the lake from us that would draw us into this horror story and would cost us our lives. No, that's not right, it did cost two of us our lives and you know who they were.

It was one of those freak things that happen once in a while, something that none of the three of us had realized we had done. It was totally by accident and once we discovered what had happened it was too late. It was a simple, no a rather complex shoot and we had to make sure everything remained stable.

The real issue was trying to get the shots as fast as possible so that the full scope of the scene did not change from one side to the other. That was the real hard part and so we used three cameras and took shots one after the other as fast as we could move and set the cameras.

We saw nothing that would indicate that something bad was taking place. We saw the cars across the lake parked by the water and one boat in the water just down from the cars. That was it, that's all we could see. We had to be nearly fifteen hundred feet from the parked cars and on top of that we heard nothing. We had tried to tell those guys that but they were convinced that we had taken their pictures and wanted our film.

Meanwhile, across the lake on the boat, the one remaining man, Gee, saw the three men on the bank across from him and they had cameras. He turned to the three security guards on shore and pointed across the lake at the men. "Get their film by any means you must, but get their film now."

When Gee gave an order there were no alternatives. The order would be carried out even unto the death of whomever and how many that was necessary. The security men would come back with the film one way or the other.

Gee had just finished a most unpleasant duty in the execution of a traitor to the Gilgon command and especially to Commander Gaa. The officer Zdd had broken a most important rule within the ranks of the Gilgon military. A rule so important, that only one single act of misconduct in regards to that rule meant death.

Zdd had developed a relationship with an Earth based female. Emily was aware of Zdd's status as an alien and that made no difference to her. It was a quiet sunny day six months earlier when she was walking the city park in White Plains, New York. Actually, she ran headlong into this huge man that was standing there in the park watching a crowd of people across the street.

She didn't cause much damage to him other than landing on her butt right there in front of him. He stood there looking down at her and then reached down and picked her up and held her at arm's length, looking her straight in the eyes. "You can put me down now, please."

He didn't make a move. "Please, I'm sorry for hitting you I wasn't paying any attention to where I was going."

He slowly let her down on her feet and then asked. "What's your name?"

Normally she wouldn't have struck up a conversation with a stranger but this man had a warm and magnetic air about him. She smiled. "My name is Emily, what's yours?"

He looked beyond her and then back at her and replied. "My name is Zdd."

Emily stood there looking at him. She had never heard a name like that before and it struck her that it didn't match his physic. "Zdd? That's an odd name."

He smiled at her. "Well to me Emily is an odd name too."

Finally, he stopped glancing across the street and asked. "Emily, how would you like to go and have a cup of coffee with me?"

Now Emily never did anything with someone she had no idea as to who he or she was, what they did or where they lived. Yet this man was not the normal man. There was something about him that reached into her and drew her to him. She liked him right off and that was strange to say the least. Emily never socialized with men. Then she did something totally out of character. "I would love to have a cup of coffee with you."

That was the start of their relationship together. Within twenty-four hours they spent their first night together and as a result Emily was madly in love with Zdd. It was not long after that when he told her the truth. Her lover was an alien and if his comrades or command found out about it, they would both die. "Zdd you're telling me that if this Gaa finds out that you and I have been making love together he would see that I was killed and you would die as well?"

It was then that he knew he had done something unforgivable to Emily. He had sealed her fate, if Gaa found out. Yet he couldn't help it he had to see her and he had to have her. The amazing thing about it was that she felt the same way. And so, they spent the next six months giving of themselves to one another.

They knew they couldn't keep it a secret forever. Then finally one day it happened, completely by accident. One of his fellow Gilgons saw Zdd enter Emily's house and that started the downfall of the two lovers.

Three days later as Zdd and Emily lay together in Emily's bed. The door to the bedroom slowly opened and in walked Gee. Nothing was said by either side. Zdd stood up and placed himself between Gee and Emily and asked Gee. "Leave her be. She'll tell no one. This was my fault and I am willing to face the consequences, so leave her out of it.

Gee snapped his fingers and two more Gilgons entered the room and walked over and took Zdd by the arms and walked him out of the room. As they left, he looked back. "Emily I'm sorry I never wanted it to end this way."

Up to this point Emily had not made a sound. She knew full well what was coming and she wasn't going to disgrace Zdd. She looked at Gee. "Before you kill me, I want you to know that I love Zdd deeply and that I am more than willing to die for him. He is the most wonderful being I have ever met and the past six months have been the most wonderful time of my life."

She then turned her head away from Gee as he pulled his gun out and placed it against the side of her head. Just before pulling the trigger, he leaned over to her. "I understand. He is a good man and I'm sure he found himself a good woman but we have rules and we must live by them."

He pulled the trigger and Emily fell back on the bed. Gee stood there watching the white of the bedding change to red. In better times Zdd would have lived a wonderful life with this woman, but not now.

That was one of the prime rules that no Gilgon violated. When discovered it meant the immediate death of the female, which had already been carried out, and the execution of the violating Gilgon.

Gee had known Zdd most of their lives and it troubled him to have to carry out the execution, but if he failed then it would mean his life as well. Zdd knew the situation that he had placed Gee in and when they came for him, he did not resist. He had thought that he could get by with the relationship and had been successful for six months, but then he got careless and was observed by one of his fellow officers.

By duty that officer had to report the situation to Gee and that resulted in her death and Zdd being taken into custody. What a price to pay for six months of love and enjoyment with one another. It did not hurt that much for him to face death, but it hurt so much more seeing her die for his transgression. For that alone he deserved to die.

So Zdd had died and the earth men had gotten pictures of the actual execution or let's say they may have gotten some pictures of the actual act. Whether those beings lived or died would depend on whether they surrendered their film or tried to resist his men, either way they would recover the film and the matter would be dead, literally.

I have no doubt now that we would have been killed right then and there if providence had not sent a life saver to our rescue. We were just knocking our cameras down and loading the car up when that

Cadillac pulled up by our car and three of the biggest guys I had ever seen got out of the car.

These guys would make any guard or tackle in the NFL look like kiddies; they were that big. When they walked up to us, they were friendly and asked what we were doing. Jacob told them that we were taking photos for a panoramic scene we had been planning for some time.

Finally, the lead guy looked at all three of us. "Look fellas we don't want to be a problem for you but we have a boss that is rather sensitive about having his picture taken and if there is even the slightest possibility that someone had taken his picture, he wants it stopped and the film taken."

He stopped for a second and let that sink in and then continued. "Now he is more than willing to pay you for the film and your time spent taking the photos and so that is why we are here. I want to request that you turn your film over to us and we will pay you for your time and costs and be on our way."

The three of us were standing there looking at each other and Ty stepped forward. "Look guys we don't want any trouble either, but we have been working on this job for months and frankly are not willing to throw it all away just like that. No, we have worked hard on this project. Thank you for the offer, but our answer is no."

The three of them looked at each other and then Ty went down. It was so fast that I had not seen the punch that hit him. All I knew was that he was down and out for the count. The three of them then turned toward Jacob and me and with that we picked up our cameras, opened them and handed the film over to the leader. He looked down at our cases and waited, we complied.

What they didn't know, and would ultimately result in our being pursued and my friends being killed, was that one of the cameras, mine, had a digital card in it and I failed to pull that for them. They asked for our film and I gave it to them. Nothing was said about cards or any other form of image storage.

When they were satisfied with the results, one of them walked over to me and took my hand and placed an envelope in it. He then patted me on the cheek and told me that cooperation always ends in a good way. "Tell your friend there on the ground that he needed to learn that lesson and in the future things won't go that hard on him."

One of the three then made a grunt and nodded his head in the direction toward the south end of the parking lot. I looked that way and spotted a Sheriff's patrol car slowly cruising toward us. They turned and walked back to the Cad and left the way they came. As they turned back onto the road and headed back for the other side of the lake Jacob and I went to help Ty.

As Ty came around his whole jaw was swollen to about twice its normal size. He sat there holding his jaw and looking at us. By this time, it was already starting to blacken up and look like the hell it must have felt like. I leaned toward him. "Are you going to be all right? Do you want to go to a hospital?"

He looked at me with a freaking stupid expression on his face and shook his head no. He then slowly and carefully said. "No, I'll go see my doctor when we get home. Right now, all I want to do is go home and lay down and I'll worry about the doctor tomorrow."

I looked at him. "All right we'll get you home."

I turned to Jacob. "Come on let's get everything in the car and get the hell out of here."

I looked over toward the patrol car and it had turned around and was leaving the parking lot and heading away from us. You would have thought that the deputy would have seen us and one of us on the ground, but evidently he didn't.

The thing that was really eating at me was the speed in which that guy had thrown that punch. I didn't even see it. All I could tell was that Ty said something and then he was down and out. When I asked Ty about the punch, he told me that he never saw it coming. He remembered telling the guy no and then waking up lying on the ground.

We had missed something and I couldn't figure out what it was. There had to have been a punch thrown, but one that was so fast neither Jacob and I nor Ty saw it.

It took us less than ten minutes to finish loading up my car and heading home. I thought about going to the police but thought I had better ask the others first. "You think we should report this to the police?"

Jacob looked at me and started shaking his head. "Hell no, did you see the size of those guys and I can assure you that there are others behind them. If we report this and they happen to be arrested then I would suspect that we would have additional visitors in the not-too-distant future and we would really find ourselves in hot water."

Ty nodded his head as well and I let the issue drop. I was sure that I wanted to report it, but the two of them were against it and that was all there was to it. It was over and we would continue living our lives having learned a rather important lesson. Know what you're shooting before taking the shot.

We got Ty home and into his house and then went our separate ways. When I got home I pulled out the equipment and took it into the house, then grabbed my camera and opened it up and pulled out the photo card. I put the card in my computer's card reader and loaded the photos up on the monitor and then sat back and looked at the series of pictures we had taken to make the panorama.

I was curious about the man who had sent those three after us I wanted to see what he looked like. As I scanned the series I came to the middle of the group and stopped at the three middle shots. I blew the first one up and noted there was nothing there except the back

40

end of a boat. I then blew the middle one up and froze.

These things just don't happen, but it did to me and this was one photo that was going to cost me and the other two our lives if it got out that I had it. I sat there looking at the blow up of the photo. It was the center portion of the boat with a man standing back of the rail looking directly out and across the lake toward us. He had this blank look on his face with his eyes squinting. What the hell kind of an expression was that?

Next to him was another man who looked to be in his mid-forties and dressed in an expensive suit. He was standing there turned ninety degrees to my camera position and about three feet from the man facing us. The suited dude had a gun to the other man's head with the barrel about a foot from the man facing us.

I could see the smoke from the barrel between the muzzle of the gun and the man's head. That was to my right. On the left side I could see the spray coming from the side of his head as the bullet passed on through that man's head. It was a cloud of blood and whatever. Even at that distance the details were stunning.

Oh God. Ah man. We had taken the perfect picture of a murder in progress. Just as the killer, in the suit, pulled the trigger and the round hit the man's head and got to the other side, I had shot the photo. Man, this could get us all killed and probably would. I was sure that I was going to be sick. I sat there looking at the guys face and again seeing his squinting eyes. My eyes were drawn down to his hand and I noted how they were gripping the railing of the boat; he was hanging on for dear life.

I then backed the view away so that I could see more of the photo and when I did that, I noted that there were others on the boat and standing just behind the victim. Sure, as hell it was two of the guys who had come over to visit us. I sat there looking at that photo knowing damn well that I was looking at the cause of my own death, yet there was something there that drew my attention.

I didn't know or recognize what it was at first, but I knew it was there. It was in plain sight, yet I was not seeing it. I was looking at four men standing on this boat with one of them standing square onto the railing and holding on for dear life. It was that man, what was it about him that I was not getting. Look damn it look, you have to see it.

It was maybe forty or fifty seconds later that it hit me. His hands, it was his hands. There were only three fingers on both hands. The detail was grainy for a shot that far out, but the computer was compensating well for it, and sure enough, it was the hands that were out of place. Three fingers and they were perfectly formed and it was clear that there had never been a fourth finger on those hands. That's the way they came, with just three fingers.

I then shifted to the hand holding the gun. There it was he had three fingers and a thumb. My guts started rolling as the realization of what I was seeing started to bury itself in my mind. They're not human.

It had been two days since we got home and I felt the need to call Ty. No answer, nothing at all. He had to be there; the dumb bastard was in too much pain to be out running around. I hung up the phone and sat there trying to think.

The whole picture started to run through my mind again. We had been to the lake, taken our photos, had the situation with those men and then came home. After getting home I had gone to the bank the next day, Monday, and withdrawn all my funds. Why the hell had I done that anyway? I looked over at the table and there it was all stacked neatly on the table, every cent I owned.

Just then my phone rang and when I answered it was Jacob and he was nearly screaming at me. "They killed Ty and they're after us. Damn-it Peter you should have given them everything. I just want you to know I'm getting the hell out of here and I would advise you to do the same?'

Before he hung up, I heard a loud crash and then heard Jacob cry out. "No please. Pete, they're not human." There was almost an animal roar and then it was silent.

I grabbed everything I could get my hands on and headed out the door to my car and left the area. I drove north for maybe an hour to get out of the area and give me time to think. Somehow, they knew about the data card and where we were at. How the hell did they know that?

I then realized that I had taken a dramatic move when I withdrew my money and took it home with me. Why had I done that I don't know, but I do know that it was most timely and exactly want I needed to do.

In addition, I had come to believe, and would later confirm this, that those beings would have come to kill us anyway and not because I kept that photo card, but because they wanted to eliminate any possible relationship to the three of us, and they would do that by killing us.

Not humans? For the love of God what is going on. Not humans, then what or who are they and what had we walked into anyway. What was Jacob looking at when he yelled that out? What had he seen that made him blurt that out? He sounded terrified and he must have died in a state of pure terror as well.

All I knew at this time was that I needed to get the hell out of Dodge and do it now and the only place I could go was west, as far west as I could run in as fast a time as I could manage. I had only one thing that was in my favor and that was the fact that I had the picture. With that I had something to bargain with and it could be the one thing that would save my life. I had no idea that this was going to be a long and drawn-out situation. Damn, if I had only given them that card.

Chapter Three

SALTON SEA SANCTUARY

As I said before the rest of the run to the west coast was no big deal except for the fruit thing. Right now, as I swung onto I-15 still west bound, I had to determine where I wanted to be. That is, did I want a high population density or a more laid back and less populated area? I had to make up my mind, I was only around an hour from the L.A. area and I needed to know what I was going to do.

In a densely populated area, it was easier to get lost, but it was also full of danger of being found out. As you walk the streets of that part of the state of California there are all kinds of people moving around you. It's literally mind boggling and you're totally vulnerable to those hunting you. I decided to go for the lower populated areas and found the first road south toward the Salton Sea area. It didn't occur to me at the time as to why I decided to head for the Salton Sea area, I just did, or so I thought.

The Salton Sea is located about eighty-five miles due east of San Diego and thirty-five miles due north of Mexicali, Mexico. It is primarily a recreational area with scores of resorts located near and around the Sea itself.

The Sea came into being in 1905 when the Colorado River flooded the Imperial Valley right on the San Andreas Fault. It is actually two hundred twenty-six feet below sea level, yet its deepest part is still five feet higher than Death Valley.

As I drove south, I became more convinced that this was the place I needed to be. It was out of the way and separated from the mass of population in Southern California. This would give me the time to sit down and work my way through all that had happened and hopefully forge a new life in this place.

There was a mass of questions that needed to be addressed. The answers, I had no idea if I would come up with them. I needed time to sit down and slowly go over each and every action and event and try to come up with some idea as to just what has happened and who I am dealing with. I also needed to learn everything I could about Ty and Jacob.

I finally settled into a small town named Seeley, which was located just two miles southwest of the El Central Naval Base, home of the Blue Angels precision flying team. Seeley is part of the El Central Metro Area and is a town of about one thousand seven hundred thirty-nine, correct that to one thousand seven hundred forty with my moving in. It was also twenty-two miles south of the Salton Sea.

This placed me in an area that gave me access to the larger metro areas as well as shelter me from them. I felt that it would be relatively easier for spotting strangers coming into town than if I were in the more populated areas. In addition, I had a feeling that the close proximity to the El Central Naval Base would also give me an advantage. I didn't know how as yet, but there was something there that gave me the impression it was an advantage for me.

The other side of that advantage was that I had fairly easy access to the metro areas as well. San Diego was only eighty-five miles west and Los Angeles was one hundred seventy miles northwest of Seeley. Phoenix was two hundred fifteen miles east and Las Vegas was two hundred twenty-eight miles northeast. That gave me a fairly easy running time to any of these larger areas and also gave me access to being lost in the masses if and when that came about.

Money wise I was in good shape in that I had cleaned out my bank accounts on the second day after returning from the trip to the lake.

Why did I do that? I really don't know. I thought I was changing banks but maybe I wasn't. Anyway, after our run in with those guys I was more than happy to have the money with me. I guess I needed to move the money to a better location or whatever so I took the precautions of withdrawing my funds and taking them home. All in all, I had around three hundred thousand, give or take twenty or thirty thousand. That wouldn't last me many years, but it gave me enough if I was frugal and watched myself.

I sat there thinking about what had driven me to withdraw my money. It didn't make sense that I would go down and withdraw it all and take it home. I had no idea of the coming events and I surely did not figure my two best friends would end up dead. What the hell was going on anyway? Then to cap it all off I have driven all the way across the country and had not thought of that until this moment.

I needed to figure this thing out and do it now, but I found myself stumped. I was confused and scared and clearly had been doing things that now seemed to be more than a little strange. Anyway, I was there and that was the end of it so I might as well start living my new life.

I felt I needed a minimum of a year to work my way through this happening to try and determine who these people were and why they were there in the first place. I had lost my two best friends and knew that if they killed Ty and Jason, they would be tracking me and planning the same fate.

As I pulled into Seeley, I started looking for apartments or a single-family house that was for rent. Nothing fancy, just a nice quiet location, you know small families with little or no partying. Within a couple of hours, I found just the right location and was able to get the apartment I wanted and I was ready to move in.

It was a small one-bedroom apartment located in a small complex. It was a town house at the far back end of the facility in a rather private and quiet area. I was in the end unit. The next thing I needed was the furnishings and so I set out to find what I needed.

Almost six hours later I returned just when the first delivery van pulled up. Everything went fine after that; I received the last of my furnishing the following morning just after nine o'clock. I had already set up a computer and printer in one corner of the dining area and had gotten on line and started my research. I would be spending a good part of my time on that machine and looking into the whole of this situation I had found myself in.

Oh, the issue with the fruit? It's still there and I have to have a fairly large amount of fruit on hand continuously or else I start having problems. What problems? I'll cover that later.

My research started with our photo trip which resulted in all the trouble with the three strangers. That photo trip had been planned for several weeks and involved an attempt at a panorama photo shoot at a small lake in northwestern New York State. It was Chazy Lake located in the Adirondack Mountains.

It's located just outside the town of Dannemora, New York. It is one of those lakes where people-built vacation lodges all around the lake and actually turned it into a private lake for their needs. There are some lake access points and we had selected one at the end of the Welfred King Road. It has a park located right on the lake called the Adirondack Park Preserve. Directly across the lake from that park was the Chazy Lake Beach, another public access point.

We selected this location because of the fact that the park sat in an inlet so when we started the shot, we would come off of land to the west of us that juts out into the lake and then sweeps around for a full one hundred eighty degrees to another point on the east side that juts into the lake. The actual area of the lake covered would come to about one hundred twenty degrees with the rest being the two points and the homes on them.

We wanted the sun behind us and so we had selected a morning shoot. In order to get set up for that time of the morning we had planned our run up to the lake the day before.

Why all this for just a photo? Well, it was not just the photo but the process of getting that photo. If everything came together then the resulting photo could become famous and possibly worth a considerable amount of money.

The town of Dannemora was located southeast of the lake and near the State of New York Penitentiary named the Clinton Correctional Facility. This meant that a large number of the people living in Dannemora were state employees working at the penitentiary. At this point I'm not sure if this facility has anything to do with what we witnessed and eventually cost two lives and my running for my life. But I needed to keep it under consideration.

We stayed in Plattsburgh at a local motel thirteen miles from Dannemora and eighteen miles from the lake. On that particular morning we had stopped off and had a great breakfast before heading up to the lake and our photo session. As we came into the park at the water's edge the weather was perfect. The sky was clear and dark blue and that gave the lake a deep blue color. With the contrast of the green forests around the lake we were sure to get great shots.

It took more time to set up than it did to shoot the photos, but we took our time and made sure we did it all right the first time. We wanted no screw ups. We had been planning this shoot for weeks and needed it to go off like clockwork. From our position it was less than half a mile across the lake.

They say the water is so clear you can drink it straight out of the lake. I doubted that, but it was clearer than any lake I had ever seen before.

That morning there was only one boat visible on the lake from our position. It appeared to be about half way out in the lake and was just sitting there. It was around thirty feet long and was what you would call a 'Cigarette' boat or 'Go Fast' boat. I noticed the boat and thought to myself that it was a rather small cigarette, but it sure looked good.

There were four men on the boat and at the time we pulled up the boat appeared to be sitting there and resting in the water, not going anywhere just sitting. I remember looking across the lake to the public beach on the other side and saw a truck with a trailer and then two other long low black vehicles sitting next to the truck.

There were a number of people standing around on the shore. There was nothing really different about the scene, just a boat with two guys in it standing at the rail and then a couple of men standing back of them and others standing around the towing vehicle on shore.

We had finally finished setting the tripods up and in the process of mounting the three cameras when I noticed that the boat was cruising toward the other side of the lake, toward the beach boat launch. There was little if any wake and the boat couldn't have been going more than a mile an hour. It was just cruising toward shore.

As I thought and recalled all the details the best I could, I was busy entering that information into the computer. I remember the boat had moved to within five hundred feet of the launch as we continued working to setup the photo session. We finally finished the setup and started to take the pictures. Each of us took our turn.

First Ty, and as he took each photo, he spotted markers along the line of shooting so that he could reposition the camera for the next shot. When Ty finished, I then made my shoot. Ty pulled his camera down and moved out of the way. I was three feet further back from the water and then I took my run of shots.

When I finished Jacob did his and once, he was done we were ready to break the equipment down and head for the motel. While taking the shots we hadn't noticed any sound or action from the boat. It was just sitting there. I had noticed that both the men in the boat had been standing as I moved into position to shoot my turn. When Jacob finished, I noticed the boat was heading in to the launch area and thought nothing of it.

It was ten minutes later when our visitors pulled up and confronted us over the film in our cameras. I needed to slow down now and try to remember every second of that encounter. I was sure it was going to be important and I needed to get it all down and down right.

The car was a dark brown Cadillac with New York state plate. It was a four door and was probably a newer model STS, about a 2008. It was well kept and stood out with all the windows darkened.

I remember three men exited the vehicle, one from the rear driver's side and then two from the front. The one that got out of the rear seat was the one that approached us and requested our film, later demanding it. The other two stood back and seemed to be more interested in the areas around us and behind them. I noticed that they kept their hands behind their backs as did the man walking up to us.

As I said before, he was a big man around six and a half feet tall and had to weigh in around two hundred fifty pounds. The other two matched that size almost perfectly. Come to think of it they all had the same haircuts and their hair was brown, a dark brown in color. Their hair was cut short I guess what you would call a Butch cut.

The one talking to us, had penetrating eyes, that were a deep gray. Yes, they were gray. I had never in my life seen someone with gray eyes. The other thing about the eyes, I had not noticed before until now that is, they couldn't hold still. I mean they were moving up and down and around and at the time of our meeting I had thought how the hell he could see with all that movement going on.

His nose was nothing unusual nor was his lips. It then hit me that his teeth were odd in some way. I got up and went to the bathroom and stood there looking in the mirror and opening and closing my mouth. What was it about his teeth and his mouth, there was something but what was it?

I stood there looking at my image in the mirror trying to determine what it was that was bothering me. As I opened and closed my mouth one last time it hit me. His teeth, they were smaller and set apart from each other nothing like our teeth.

I hadn't noted that before, but in the sudden change of action when Ty was hit, I forgot about the guys teeth and concentrated on what he was saying and having us do. The guys facing us were not like any other people I had ever seen, either in person or in the news or other documents. It was starting to register in my mind that these men were unlike any on earth.

Then add the fact that the two on the boat both had the same basic appearance as the three we faced and those two had only three fingers on both their hands. I was coming to the conclusion that, considering all that I had seen, I was sure that I was looking at people that were not of this world, and if they were not people of this world then they had to be something else, a something I didn't want to say.

It then struck me, aliens? No, that couldn't be, those are stories that come out of fiction and have nothing to do with reality. Yet, there it was, five men that I saw and all five had the same traits and appearance that were not of this world.

The tears started to run down my face as I grappled with the thought of aliens being here in our world. The full impact of that idea was starting to settle in on me and my heart started to fill with terror.

What the hell had we stumbled onto anyway? If those people, well that one individual, were in fact killing that other person and they were alien and the victim was alien then what would we here on this earth care anyway, unless they don't want us to know that they are in fact here.

It then dawned on me that it was probably not the picture that was the problem, but the fact that on that picture we could identify that the people were not of this earth, that they were alien. Now they had two reasons for tracking me down and removing me.

I guess it was all too much because I must have passed out at the computer and fell to the floor. I was awake almost as soon as I hit the floor and I laid there trying to regain a sense of understanding and control within my mind. It just couldn't be true, yet there it was. To be specific, it defies any other interpretation, they had to be alien.

I had read stories and seen television reports about people who have claimed to see alien space craft and then those who claimed to have been abducted, yet none of it rang true. It was all a bunch of hysterics and now I'm one of them. No, that's not true. I'm not one of them, our story is different and we have two dead people to support that fact. The bottom line was, whether alien or not, they were after me.

They had killed my two best friends. They had killed one of their own out there on that lake that morning, for what reason I have no idea. And now they were going to try to deal with me. I had the picture; I witnessed the killing and I was running from them. My head was swimming with thoughts and fears all at the same time. I knew that I wouldn't stand a chance with them on my own. But where was I to get help, and if I found someone would they actually help me.

No, my situation was different and it was beyond anything this world had seen or anticipated. What were they here for? Were they here to invade and take over? Was the human race facing its end?

There were all kinds of questions going through my mind as I lay there on the floor letting my mind charge through all the possibilities. One thing was for sure I had better get my act together and go to work and figure this out. There were answers out there and I needed to find them and find them fast.

Chapter Four

THE SUPERSTITIONS

I found it hard to believe that any form of alien life could have landed here on earth and no one would have known anything about it. If that were true then there had to be groups out there who were aware of their presence and were trying to deal with it. It was then that I knew I had to find some of those groups and get their help.

I felt that any of the well-known and publicly active groups were of no help. They had made themselves unbelievable over the ways in which they have pursued this issue and their willingness to accept and support just about anyone's ideas or concept whether believable or not. No, there are groups out there who are working quietly behind the scenes and it's those people that I need to find.

So, I had two search criteria already, I was looking for any and all information on alien sightings around the world that matched with what my friends and I had witnessed. The second was the search for a bonafide and active group who were also trying to deal with this issue. If there were any other issues, I would include them as I found them.

I got up off the floor and sat back down in front of the computer and let my body get back into a functioning mode. The stress was more than I had ever been faced with and the fact that I passed out told me just how hard it was hitting my body. All I could do was sit and wait and let things work them out. If I was going to really make an impact and do something about this, I was going to need to get control of myself and do it now.

It dawned on me that I had not eaten all day and it gave me an idea. I needed to eat and research my problem. At the same time I have this craving for fruit of any kind. All were related in one way or the other and that gave me the idea to combine all my activities, seeing if it gave me any insight into the issues

I was pursuing. I got up and went to the kitchen and worked up a sandwich and a bowl of fruit and then returned to the computer and started to eat and search the web.

The fruit, that was one of the keys, why was I so addicted to fruit, I could not understand that. Maybe if I started my search there it would give me some path to jump onto and follow. The question, "What causes my addiction to fruit in the first place?

There had to be something that kicked this addiction off and then it hit me. I still had not checked on what had happened to Ty and Jacob.

It has been weeks since I ran from New York that early morning, and I had not checked to see if there was anything on their deaths. I started the research on the two of them and finally found the information I wanted. It was buried in the local section of the papers and was addressed as homicide investigations. I started reading and almost immediately the paper had tied the two of them together as friends.

The papers had tied into that relationship and as a result the articles were fairly detailed and extensive. Both bodies had been found in the bedroom of their respective apartments. They had been killed by a large caliber weapon one big enough to blow their entire chest cavity out.

As the police inspected their home, they found a profusion of fruits from simple grapes to bananas, apples, oranges, guavas, lemons, grapefruit, pineapples, strawberry's and many others. There were indications that they both had been eating an excessive amount of fruit throughout their apartments. Though this was not something that they felt addressed the killings it was considered unusual.

As I read through the articles, I noted that it appeared both men had been killed in their living room areas and then taken into the bedrooms. There was no apparent reason for that action in that the bodies had no other damage beyond the wounds made at the time they were killed. One would have thought that they would have been taken in the bedroom for a reason such as to be interrogated but there was no indication of any other action.

The story continued about both men, it had been determined that they had been close friends and had just come back from a trip up into northwestern New York State. It was also determined that a third friend of theirs, a Peter

Danials, was also missing and the authorities had no idea as to where he might be.

Upon being asked if this Mr. Danials was a suspect in the death of the other two the investigators advised that everyone was a suspect until proven not to be. Great now I'm suspected in the killing of my buddies.

Little else was available in the articles at that time and then it came to me, what about the man that had been killed on the lake that day when we had the confrontation with the three thugs. I looked up the area news for Dannemora and found nothing. In fact, a complete search of the entire area of the Adirondack Mountain areas had nothing on any death or even an assault.

After that search I then went back to Ty and Jacobs's death and zeroed in on the fruit issue. Both had been eating a considerable amount of fruit, as was I. I knew when we had gone to the lake none of us had that kind of an issue. We had stopped for lunches and breakfasts and dinners and no one had ordered fruit at any of those meals. Yet, all three of us had a need for fruit. What was the link? How did it happen?

It occurred to me that it must have been while we were at the lake and shooting our pictures. If that was the case then the only thing out of the ordinary that took place was the confrontation with the three strangers. I centered in on that meeting and ran it over and over in my mind. What happened that would cause us to all become fruit addicts.

Ty had been knocked flat on his back by a punch that was so fast and so hard I failed to see it thrown, but I knew it had been thrown. Then the leader had turned to me and I gave up the film and he then reached out and patted me on the cheek and actually pinched my cheek. I hadn't remembered that until now.

As he turned and walked back toward his car he stopped at Jacob and reached out and patted his cheek and I now remember that he pinched Jacob's cheek as well. I ran that over in my mind again and again. Ty was hit in the cheek and then Jacob and I were patted and pinched on the cheek. Slowly it dawned on me.

They had tagged us. They had marked us for future location and if that is true then they know damn well where I am right now and what I'm doing. But, if they did then why have they not come after me to take me out?

The picture! Yes, it had to be the picture. They can't kill me, I'm the only one who knows where the picture is and I may have set things up so that it would find its way into the hands of the authorities. That could be costly to them.

All right, so far, I've determined that when we had the one-on-one contact with the men at the lake, they had tagged us in some way. The craving for the fruit clearly indicates that is what happened. I had withheld the photo data card from them along with a set of pictures of the killing.

The identity of the men on the boat was out there somewhere. I had the photos and they did not know just where those photos were. That was my cover, my protection. They had to know where all the pictures were and, in some way, find and collect them before dealing with me. Damn was I in a pickle of a situation.

By this time, I was at a standstill. I really had no idea as to which way to go nor did I have any idea as to how to get something moving in any direction. In the past I had learned that if I took a walk or a drive and let things settle down, I would come up with answers to whatever it was I was dealing with. So, I went out to my car and headed out into the back country of the southeastern region of California. I had no idea where I was going, I just needed to drive and think.

I actually headed northwest of Seeley and passed the United States Naval Air Base located just north of my place. I drove about fourteen miles out into the desert to the base of the Superstition Mountains and found a spot and parked.

I got out and was looking up at the mountains when it started to come to me. It turned out to be simple and complex at the same time. I needed to trace the history of unusual deaths around the New York State area and then start to match those kinds of deaths and situations to the deaths of my two friends to determine what similar issues were involved. The search of the history and archives of that area would be no problem. It was a way to develop the foundation I was looking for.

I had a lost feeling standing there at the foot of the Superstitions realizing that I was all alone in this. As I looked up at those barren drab-colored mountains a feeling started to settle over me. There was something familiar about that region and I had no idea how this could be. I had never been in this place, and yet it was familiar. I had heard of the Superstitions and all of the folklore that surrounded this place.

Then there were the Indian cultural stories that were all over the place. These mountains were the place of great supernatural meaning to the natives of this region. Somehow, in some way, this place meant something to me. It was probably the strangest feeling I had ever had in my life. The more I stood there looking, the more I knew this place had meaning to me, but just what that was I could not begin to guess.

Off to the east was the Salton Sea and to the west were the coastal mountains. Here in between it was barren sand covered desert, except for those mountains. I started to turn and walk back to the car when I felt this need to look back. As I did, I caught the glint of sun light flashing off a shiny surface like a mirror or lens of a camera or something like that. I stood there looking at it and after several seconds it dawned on me it was not moving but was actually holding a steady orientation on me.

Hell, it could have been anything, a tourist looking through his binoculars, a photographer scanning for a good shot, a car or truck windshield, any number of things that just happen in areas like this. As I got into the car and headed further west, I approached the northern most part of the mountains and then pulled over and stopped again. As I got out of the car a flash of light hit my eyes and I saw the same flicker I had seen four miles back. Whoever it was had decided to concentrate on me, for what reason I had no idea.

It was then I decided I needed to leave and made a mental note to do some research on this area. Why, I had no idea but something told me I had to do that and I had to do it tonight, as soon as I got back to my place. As I headed back to Seeley, I had an overwhelming feeling that those mountains meant something, and it was important.

An hour later, after stopping off and getting some chicken and a large drink at a nearby fast-food place, I was at my computer typing in the Superstition Mountains and hitting search. As I waited for the search to be completed, I started thinking about the actual size of these mountains and the area where they were located. It was not that large an area, land wise.

The mountain range itself is only about six miles long running from the northwest to the southeast. They sit in an area that is roughly twenty by twenty-five miles of fairly flat desert country, clearly separated from any other major geological structure.

Was it any wonder that the natives of this region saw those mountains as something special? They are old, separated from the other mountain ranges in that part of the state, and that gave them a special appearance.

I knew I needed to delve into their history and its relationship to those regions of the state. There was something there that demanded my attention. In time I would learn more than I ever wanted to know and the reality that will come from it will change my life and the lives of every man, woman, and child that lived in this area.

The result of my computer search on the Superstitions was into the millions of hits. As I sat there looking at all the hits, I began to see something odd, the descriptions of the mountains I had been too did not match and I noticed that they referenced Arizona. That was odd.

Then it hit me there was another Superstition Mountain and it was located in

Arizona, not far from Apache Junction. A check of the map showed me the relationship of these other Superstitions to the area around them. They were much bigger and ran south to north.

They were the mountains that had all the history and stories of the Dutchman's mine. No, these Superstition Mountains in Arizona were something else altogether. I had been mistaken about the local California Superstitions they were not the ones I thought they were.

The California Superstition Mountains were well visited by ATV riders because of its many sand dunes and mountain trails. But there was something else about the place that stood out. There was a feeling as I stood there, at the base of the mountains, and looked up at its barren slopes. It was a feeling I had never felt before and one that was growing in intensity. It then came to me I needed to take a trip to the southeast and the other Superstitions.

She had been to the Superstitions just outside of Seeley at least four times before and needed to be there again. Why, she had no idea but she had to go. From the time she had left Florida to now she felt that she was not alone and that there was something waiting for her.

She had just gotten back from the Arizona Superstitions and the Apache Junction area and now she was back out to the California Superstitions. She was looking for something, but what that was she had no idea all she knew was that she had to keep coming back, keep looking.

I set to work on a plan to take a trip to the Phoenix area and ultimately to the Arizona Superstition Mountains. I had no idea as to how long I was going to be gone and so I set my plans to be open ended. After all, I had no place to go, no work or job to report to and no one who depended on me. I could be gone as long as I needed.

But first I had one thing that needed to be done right now. I returned to the computer and set about printing out several pictures of the events that took place in New York State. In all I did five sets of pictures and then placed each set in an envelope and sealed them. I then located four banks in El Centro and also a park that had a lot of space and structure to it.

My plan was to deposit a copy of each set of pictures in four separate bank safety deposit boxes and leave them there. The fifth set was to be placed somewhere in the park. I had no idea where at the time, but would make that determination when I got to the park.

Next, I found the names of four attorneys in El Centro and called each one and made an appointment with them over a four-hour period where I would visit each attorney and hire them to tend to the details of my plan. Each would be left with an envelope with the key to the safety deposit box in one of the banks.

My instructions to each were that if they did not hear from me over a three-week period then they were to go to that bank and get the envelope in the safety deposit box and turn the envelope over to the federal authorities without opening the envelope themselves. I set my wrist watch to a date three weeks ahead at each attorney's office and then paid my fees and left. The hidden envelope at the park was for me in the future as I needed it.

The next morning, I headed out from Seeley and went east into El Centro and to the four attorneys' offices. I then went to the park and walked around until I found the location I wanted and placed the envelope there. I returned to my car and drove out to Interstate 10 heading for Phoenix.

I had determined that Apache Junction was on the east side of Phoenix and six miles from the Superstitions, which were east of Apache Junction. The actual Superstition Mountain Range is about thirty miles long, running south to north from Superior on the south and Saguaro Lake to the north.

This Mountain Range has a long history as a special place in the culture of the native Apache Indians. It was the focal point of their strength and the fortress of their resistance of the United States during the Indian wars. To this day they still stand as the cultural spirit of the Apache Nation and the guardian of their past.

Over the years the American social system has invaded and taken advantage of this spiritual realm of the Apache and sought out and took the treasures that the Superstitions held, namely its gold. Besides being the historical home of such great Apache leaders as Cochise of the Chiricahua tribe, Dahteste of the Mescalero tribe, Lozen of the Chiheune tribe, Mangas Colorado of the Mimbreño tribe, Victorio of the

Mimbreño tribe and Nahche of the Chiricahua tribe, it is the legacy of this noble people, the essence of all that was and is the Apache.

It was to this background that I was trying to gain an understanding of the Superstitions and to try and determine if there was any connection between the Superstitions of the Apache and the Superstitions in southern California. Physically there was no comparison. The Arizona Superstitions were clearly five times the size of the California range. There was clearly a stature to the Arizona range that had a presence, a spirit attachment that was missing in the California Mountains.

I spent four days there driving around and sitting at the foot of the Arizona Superstitions. I felt the spirit generated by the range and the lives that had passed into history in and around those peaks. It was a magical place, a place of majesty no one could fail to feel and be impacted by. There was something there that was missing in the California range and yet, the California range was the place I needed to be. I had a connection to it.

There was something here, something I could not connect with right now, but something that was going to be important to me in the near future. It was a feeling that drove itself into my mind and started to haunt me from the moment I first laid eyes on the Arizona Superstitions.

I would not make the connection for some time and when I did my world would change even more radically than it had over the past several weeks. It sent a chill through me, making my soul quiver in a way that told me things had just begun to happen.

As I left Arizona and headed back to Seeley, I could look into my rear-view mirror and see the Superstitions sitting there behind me. There was a link between the two places and I needed to find out what it was.

The other thing that was plaguing me was the question of how these two mountain ranges tied into the death of my two friends and the aliens who killed them. Yet, I knew there was a tie, a relationship, which was important to me and my survival. Where I was to go from here, I had no idea but I felt sure in short order I would know and would not like it.

She knew one thing and that was that she had to keep going out to the Superstitions and waiting and looking. She would know what she was looking for when she saw it, but for the time being she needed to keep going out there and waiting. The answer was there, all she had to do was be there and she would recognize it when she finally saw it.

Chapter Five

FINDING A PARTNER

As I said before, Seeley, California is a small town with a population of about seventeen hundred. It is located in the western side of the Imperial County just west of El Centro. The area is primarily agriculture, with a heavy dose of tourism due to the Salton Sea located on the northern end of the county.

Just two miles to the northeast of Seeley is the Navel Air Base and the home of the Blue Angels Flight Team. As I said before the Superstition Mountains are just northwest of Seeley. Interstate 8 was a short distance south of the town making access to San Diego an easy trip of eighty-six miles.

Overall, it's a pleasant community to live in with an easy lifestyle. It was the perfect place to hide out and to start my research to try and locate and deal with the aliens I have been running from.

I had returned to Seeley late that evening and had gotten a good night's sleep. The following morning, I got up around eight and took a good hot shower, spending as much time in the shower as I could. That is until I ran out of hot water. I had breakfast and while eating I started to think about the trip to Arizona and why I had these feelings or this drive to do the things I found myself doing?

I don't know why I really came here, but once I was settled in, I was then drawn to the California Superstitions and I started to wander out that way every third or fourth day as a means of trying to connect with the location and determine what it was that drew me to them. It was not the motorsports activity going on around the area almost every day. No, it was something more involved something more personal, and something more dangerous.

I also had a strong feeling there was a connection between the two different

Superstitions. I had been to Arizona and seen the Superstitions there and I knew there was a connection. Just what it was I had no idea. Hell, I didn't even understand what I was really doing, let alone making something out of it.

I was confused and getting more confused every day. One thing I knew, I had fallen into a pattern, one I couldn't break for some reason.

There was a strong feeling that she had better go back out to the Superstitions again that day. She didn't know why, but she had to go. She had known for some time that she was to find an answer there and because of that she did not fight the drive to go out there as it came on her.

It was maybe five weeks later when I found myself driving out to the Superstitions after a heavy rain had hit the area. By the time I left my place the streets were already drying up and the sun was doing its usual thing, heating everything up. As I drove across the desert, looking at those Mountains coming closer to me, I saw a strange shift in the color of the sky, just over the top of the central peak of the range. It was a subtle shift in color from the usual blue to a darker more intense blue.

At first, I thought that it was due to my movement across the desert and getting closer to the range, but the shift remained as I got closer. By the time I got to the foot hills I was convinced that there had been a shift in color, so the next question was why?

I had been out to the mountains a number of times, and during those times I had found that Huff Road was the most logical access to that area. While running Huff Road I had found two mystery circles, but I had no idea what the circles were all about, I had found them and began my research on them. At first, I thought they had been made by the ATV riders that run rampant in this area, but after looking them over I determined they were old and there was no ATV activity in or around them.

I also located two large buildings up in the actual mountains with well-kept roads leading to each building. In addition, there was a large fenced in the area to the northeast of Huff road that appeared to be currently used, but there were no indications as to what it was for and who was using it. When I got to the road leading to the fenced in area I pulled over into a flat wide area at that intersection and sat there looking at the mountain.

As I thought about those things, I had found I knew there was really nothing that would confirm those places, the circles, weren't anything suspicious or of an alien relationship. They could just as well be perfectly harmless or innocent locations that meant nothing, there was nothing to tie them together yet they were stuck in my mind. All I could do was sit there and wait, for what I had no idea.

It was a strong feeling that was coursing through her body as she drove out to Huff Road and turned onto it. She knew without a doubt that she needed to be there this day, and that it was important and it would change everything for her. The past weeks had been nothing but a haze of activity, little of which she understood. But now she was coming to a point where she was going to discover the reasons for much of what has happened.

Maybe half an hour later a vehicle came from the east on Huff Road and when it got to the intersection it too pulled off and parked about fifty to seventy-five feet away from me. The vehicle was a dark colored SUV with one occupant that appeared to be a woman. I thought nothing of it until about five minutes later when the SUV started to move toward me and then came around and drove up to my driver's window. I found myself bracing my legs and preparing to jerk the gear shifter into gear and run for it.

She saw the car parked off the road at the intersection and knew immediately that she needed to make contact. She pulled off the road into the parking area and stopped about seventy-five feet from the other car. She could see that there was a lone man in the car. The thing that scared her the most was that she knew she was going to approach that car and meet that man and she didn't know anything about who he was or what he was doing there. No, she couldn't, but she had to. She had no choice, it had to be.

As she approached my car, she opened the driver's side window and pulled up alongside me with her car pointing in the opposite direction.

I sat there looking at her and waiting for whatever was to come. She finally looked at me and then asked. "How long have you been parked here?"

I sat there looking at her. "Been here about half an hour."

She looked out her windshield as if she was trying to force herself to continue. "Did you see the change in the color of the sky?"

Now she had my attention. As I looked at her, I could see she was worried and a little scared. She seemed preoccupied with something and she was making herself talk to me. Her question had hit home and I had a feeling I needed to be responsive with this woman and see if I could learn more from her. "Yes, I saw the change and decided to stop here and watch for a while. What's your name?"

She looked at me a few seconds. "Oh, I'm sorry I wasn't thinking when I drove up to you. My name is Toni, Toni Belweather."

"Hi Toni my name is Darrel Gibson."

I reached out with my right hand and she in turn reached out and we shook hands. I noted that her hands were soft but firm. She had a good handshake, none of that softy limp kind. "Toni did you come out here because of that color change?"

She was nodding her head. "Yeah, I've been watching these mountains for the past year and this is the second time I've seen a color change like that. When I asked others, they usually scoffed at me and told me I was imagining things. But I'm not. There was a color change and it was real and it has to mean something."

I too was nodding my head. "Well Toni, I haven't been here for a year, but over the past few weeks I have learned a lot about this area and there is something going on here and I believe that color change is part of it. Just what it is I don't know yet, but I'm determined to figure it out." I stopped for a moment to give her time to assimilate what I had just said and then continued.

"I could sure use a little help from someone who knows this area and could show me around. Would you be willing to collaborate on this job?" I had just made a jump from talking to a stranger to trying to work up a working relationship with this lady and not know one damn thing about her. The fact was, it was perhaps the dumbest thing I had ever done.

Now she was looking at me like I had just proposed we jump into bed with each other. I mean she had this look on her face like she was sure I was the nut that someone had forgotten to lock away. "I don't really know you Darrel and actually I'm not sure that would be a good idea. Maybe I should just leave."

As she spoke, I started to nod my head in agreement and waited until she had finished. I then sat back in my seat and looked up at the ceiling of the car. "Look I didn't mean anything wrong when I said that. If I scared you or said something that hurt you, I apologize. I've only been in this area a few weeks and I guess I'm a little lonely and somewhat confused as to just what it is, I'm doing here anyway."

I looked over at her and she was clearly listening to me. I continued. "I have been trying to deal with my feelings about this place and so far, have made little headway. There is something about this place that is not right but I cannot tell you what it is, it's just a feeling.

"I came here from the east coast and have been trying to deal with a tragic event that took place back home, something I really do not want to talk about other than to say that I have done nothing wrong or illegal. What made me come to this location, again I have no idea. I could have gone anywhere, but I came here and I also knew this was where I had to be."

I looked at her and she too was nodding her head as I talked. She looked over at me and started to say something and then stopped and turned her head back toward the front of her car. We sat there in silence for maybe two minutes when she finally turned back to me. "You ever get that feeling that someone or something is out there waiting for you?"

The look on her face held so much fear and terror, I connected with her immediately. I recognized and knew right then and there that somehow the two of us had found one another. "Yes, I know the feeling well. It's with me day and night and never ever leaves me. Is it the same for you?"

She started to nod. "It just consumes me sometimes and I don't know why or where it came from. I end up driving out here two and three times a week hoping something would show me where I could find the answers."

I turned my head back to her and she was looking straight into my eyes and we connected. We said nothing, just sat there looking at each other and getting more uncomfortable as each second passed. "You were looking for me, weren't you?"

She sat there a few seconds and then slowly nodded her head. "Yes, I think I was and now that I've found you, what's next?"

"I don't know. I'm not even sure if it was a smart thing for us to find each other. I don't know if this is the right move or the one move that will do us both in." I was clearly scared by this time.

Things like this just don't up and happen. I had never seen this woman in my life, and yet she shows up at the exact spot I'm at with the same concerns and fears I have been dealing with all this time. I knew we needed to meet, but I also knew it was highly dangerous for the two of us to come together for whatever reason.

Finally, it came to me and I turned back to her. "I'll tell you what. There is a nice restaurant back toward town on the right side of I-80 called Juno's. You know where that is?"

She nodded in response.

"What say we both drive over there and go have something to eat while we work this out?"

She seemed to perk up at that point and agreed to meet me there. With that we nodded at one another, started our cars and headed toward Juno's.

Twenty minutes later we were walking in the front door of Juno's and looking for a secluded table where we could talk. Once we found a booth and had our menus and water, I started the conversation. "Well Toni as I said before my name is Darrel Gibson and I'm originally from New York State. I need to let you know that my name is not my real given name, which I cannot tell you at this time, but in time I hope that I can. Is that all right with you?"

She smiled and sat back. "Well Darrel as I said before my name is Toni Belweather and I come from Florida originally and that too is not my given name."

We sat there looking at each other and then I started to laugh and she followed. "I guess that makes us equals. Now where do we go from here?"

She sat forward and put her elbows on the table top. "Darrel, I'm not sure just where we should go with this thing. I know now that we needed to meet and there is something both of us are looking for and it is probably the same thing. I don't know, or I'm not sure, how we should progress from here."

I sat there turning my glass of water and wiping the moisture condensation off the outside of the glass as I turned it. My mind was running at full speed trying to come up with some way or means of moving this conversation along. We were both paranoid to some degree and for good reason, but we still had to come up with something.

Finally, I decided to take the jump. "Toni, I'm going to tell you why I'm here and what has happened to me. If at any time you feel you need to leave and end this meeting then I will accept that as a no and leave it at that. I hope to hell you understand the risk I'm taking."

She sat there saying nothing just looking me in the eyes and waiting. I noted that she was silently drumming the fingers of her left hand on the table top as she waited.

I took a deep breath and started in. "It all started several months ago when my two best friends and I decided that we wanted to take a photo trip to a lake in upper northwest New York State. The name of the lake I will not give at this time.

"We had known each other from when we were in school and one of our favorite things was photography. We spent almost every weekend on some project involving photography. Well, this particular weekend we went to this lake, we had been planning this trip for weeks and were more than just a little excited. When we got there, it was a perfect weekend. The weather was great and we had found the perfect place for shooting right off the bat. I mean nothing could have gone any better.

"On Saturday we got to the sight at just the right time and set up our equipment. We were going to shoot a panorama of the lake and had selected the perfect time and location. Anyway, we had everything set up and started taking the photos using three separate cameras so that we could match and compare when we got home.

"As we moved along taking each photo in sequence, we came to a boat sitting on the lake about five hundred feet out from the shore on the other side of the lake. I snapped a shot of the bow of the boat and then the middle and then the stern and on around completing my panorama shot.

Nothing appeared to be wrong and it all seemed like it was just the way it was supposed to be. My friends finished their swings and we were then ready to break our gear down when a car pulled into the parking area where we were.

"Three men got out of the car and came up to us and wanted our film from our cameras. Their apparent leader told us his boss did not like having someone taking his picture and that he wanted the film and that they would also pay us for the film and our time.

"One of my friends told the guy that we did not want to sell our film. He no sooner had said that when the leader hit him and knocked him out right there on the spot. They then told my other friend and me to turn the film over, which we immediately did while looking at our friend laying on the ground. At first, I thought he was dead.

"They left us standing there and we got our friend up and left the area heading for home. When they took my film, I had not told them of a photo card that was in my camera, I took that home with me. What the hell anyway, it was mine and I had worked hard setting up that shoot.

"Two days later I was home looking at the photos on the photo card. I was really looking at the boat in the photo and trying to get a good look at anyone I may have gotten

94

during the run. As I scanned the shots, I saw the stern of the boat and continued to scan along to the middle. I came across two men standing in the boat at the railing facing us.

"The first man was gripping the railing and staring out across the lake right at me. As I scanned further along, I saw a second man standing to the first man's left and ninety degrees to me. That man was about three to four feet from the first man and had his arm raised and had a gun at the side of the head of the first man.

"I could see the smoke from the barrel of the gun and when I scanned back to the first man, I saw the reddish cloud to the right of his head. The first man had been shot by the second man and I knew this was the reason those men came to collect the films from us. Hell, I had witnessed a killing and it scared the hell out of me.

"I no sooner had seen that when my phone rang and one of my friends was on the line, he was screaming at me that they were after him and they weren't human. Just then I heard his door crash in and a loud gun shot. That was all I heard and the phone went dead.

"Within minutes I was out of my place and in my car and running for my life. Over the course of several weeks, I made it out here to Seeley. Why here, I have no idea, but this is where I came and this is where I have determined that I must stay. Both my friends had been killed and I cleared out of New York and ended up here."

We sat there looking at one another and I watched the tears coming out of her eyes and running down her cheeks. I felt spent and leaned back in my seat dropping both my hands onto the table top. She reached over and placed her right hand on to the back of my left hand and held it there.

We just sat there. I had taken a risk by telling her my story and I was now waiting for whatever was to happen. Finally, she said. "A similar thing happened to me about three months ago and I'm here because this was where I came. I don't know why I came here, but I did and I've been searching for something ever since. I haven't been here for a year. The truth is it's only been about two and a half months.

"My real name is not Toni for the same reasons you are not using your real name. Maybe later on we will be able to address that issue between the two of us. Anyway, I was taking a weekend run with a couple of my friends down to Miami. It was just one of those weekends on the beach and spending some night time fun down on the strip.

"We had been night club hopping when we came across this guy who was all alone and seemed to be in need of some company. We introduced ourselves to him and he invited us to join him. There was nothing sinister about it, we just liked his looks and joined him.

"The evening went well, we took turns dancing with Tracy, which was the name he gave us, and having a great time. When it was time for the club to close, we all four walked out to the parking lot. While we were standing there talking, a car pulled up by us and two guys got out and walked around to us.

"Tracy started to back away from the two men and us and it was then when I noted their hands with only three fingers on them. The one closest to my girlfriends and I reached out and grabbed my girlfriends and pulled them to him and then shoved them in front of him and kept walking toward Tracy.

"The guy that had grabbed my girlfriends pulled a gun and put it to each one's head and pulled the trigger. I panicked and ran like hell over to a large group of people who had been watching this thing go down. The other guy then pulled a gun and shot Tracy dead right there in the lot and then they dumped my friends on top of him.

"The two men turned toward where I had run and started walking toward the crowd. At that time everyone split. There were people running all over the place and I for one was running like hell was after me. I ran to an alley and just as I started into it a hand grabbed me and literally drug me through the alley and then around a corner and pushed me behind several boxes that were stacked against the wall.

"A car with the men came driving by and the stranger stood there watching them. No one said anything, they kept going. When they were gone, he took me back to my car and told me to get the hell out of town and never come back.

"I got into my car and left Miami and then Florida and never stopped till I got here. From the moment I arrived here in Seeley I have had this continuous need to come out here to this mountain and look around. I even drove over to the Arizona Superstition Mountains to see if there was a connection between the two places and eventually determined there was no connection."

At that point I held my hand up to stop her. She stopped and sat there looking at me. "What?"

I looked hard at her. "You went over to the Arizona Superstitions?"

She nodded her head. "Yes, I did. I don't really know why, but I needed to go there and I needed to know if the two Superstitions were tied or linked in some way. Why are you asking me that?"

By this time, I was almost out of my seat. "Because I did the same thing last week, I had to go there to the other Superstitions. I didn't know why and once I was there, I felt that there was no connection, but now I think maybe there is a connection after all."

We sat there looking at one another not knowing just what to do next. Finally, she leaned across the table. "Darrel what does this all mean? What is going on here anyway?"

I sat there looking at her, letting my mind run free for a few minutes. This was either the wildest coincidence or one of the best made plans I had ever had the misfortune of experiencing. I didn't think it was coincidental and so it had to be planned, but planned by whom?

If this was planned, then it opened the door to all kinds of issues, some of which I didn't want to even consider. It came to me, were we being manipulated, and if so by whom and why? That scared me. But one thing was certain we were to be together and there was a reason for it.

I finally turned my attention back to Toni. She was clearly scared and having a hard time. I knew I had to address this thing and so I looked at her. "Toni, listen to me. This is most important. I have no doubt that we are to be together at this time. For what I have no idea, but I would bet it has to do with those people we both met in Florida and New York.

"In addition, I think we are meant to be together for a very specific reason. What that reason is, I have no idea as yet, but we were meant to meet and be together. Do you agree?"

She sat there at first doing and saying nothing and then slowly started to nod her head. She looked right at me. "I think you're right about that, we do need to be together.

The only thing that keeps coming to me still is why?"

After that we sat there in silence for the next few minutes stirring and sipping our coffees. Finally, Toni asked. "By together what do you mean?"

That, I had not thought about and it caused be to sit back and shrug my shoulders. "Really, I don't know. I feel certain that we need to be together, but I don't know what together means."

I was somewhat shaken by this time and I could feel the embarrassment settling across my face. "I think something or someone has orchestrated our coming together, but what that means and how it should play out I have no idea."

A hint of a smile crossed her face as she saw my embarrassment. "I don't think this situation meant we would end up together in a bed now, do you?"

I felt my mouth fall open and I knew I had to get up and move around but didn't know just how to get to that position. Finally, I told her. "I've got to go to the restroom I'll be back in a few minutes."

She nodded as I got out of the booth and headed for the restrooms. I needed a few minutes to think on my own. This situation was getting out of control. I had started my day heading out to the Superstitions and here I am with a woman I have no knowledge of and she just said something that caused me to almost lose it all.

Why did she have to say anything about going to bed? That hadn't even crossed my mind, but once she said it all kinds of images were flashing across my mind and none of them were what I wanted at this time.

Hell, yes, I would go to bed with her. Just take a look at her, she's great and now she's plugged the thought of bed into my head and that's all I'm seeing. Her in bed and me getting in with her, damn this is getting out of hand. I needed to clear my mind of this stuff and get back to business and what we need to do next and it's not sex.

I got back to the booth and Toni had gotten our cups refilled. As I sat down, she looked at me. "Darrel I'm sorry that I embarrassed you that way. I didn't mean to imply we had to go to bed, or that this entire situation would result in that. It was a joke and not a very good one at that."

I sat there watching her and then realized she had finished. I took a sip of coffee. "Look, you did catch me by surprise and it was a topic I had not been thinking about. It just caught me off guard, that's all." I then found myself expanding on my feelings. "Look you're a good-looking woman and frankly once I got a good look at you it did stir me somewhat."

She raised her hand. "You mean you're ready?"

"What, no wait that's not what I was saying I just said that you're a good-looking woman and I responded to seeing you and it was nothing more."

She sat there with this intense look and brushed my last statement aside. "Darrel, I repeat are you ready for me right now, right this minute?"

At that point I reached over and grabbed her by the hand. "Toni, listen to me, snap out of this, do you understand me? We are not going to become sexually involved, is that clear."

I sat there holding her hand when this shocked look crossed her face and tears started to run down her cheek. She shook her head and raised her right hand to her mouth and took a deep breath. "I don't understand why I was feeling that way and saying what I said. Oh my god, I actually wanted you to have sex with me."

I relaxed my grip as I watched her trying to deal with what had just happened. She clearly had no realization as to what she was saying and doing and that bothered the hell out of me. "Toni, listen to me, there is something going on here we do not understand.

Something or someone is trying to manipulate the two of us for some reason, what that reason is I have not the slightest idea, but it is happening and you and I have to control ourselves. Do you understand me?"

She gave me that slight smile again. "Darrel what's this all about? Don't ask me why I feel this way all I know is that I want you. Darrel I couldn't help it, I felt we had to do this, and I felt you had to come to my place with me."

She was confused and scared at the same time. She raised her hand up in front of her face and started shaking her head. "Why after only knowing you for maybe forty-five minutes would I have this feeling. I have never felt that way about a man before. What is going on?"

At this time, I was looking around the restaurant and trying to determine if there was anyone there that could be involved in this thing. I looked back at her and she was still crying and just sitting there. It dawned on me, I needed to say something to her that would calm her fears and take her off the hook. "Toni you don't have to worry about me. I realize this is something that is trying to control us and I am not going to pursue that feeling or desire, do you understand?"

She slowly nodded her head and seemed to relax somewhat. She sat there and then said something that was so totally out of left field that it took my breath away. "You mean you wouldn't go to bed with me?"

Where the hell did that come from anyway? Now she's concerned that I may be rejecting her because of something I find undesirable about her. "Toni please, listen to me, let's not get started talking about that right now. This has nothing to do with whether you appeal to me or not. Do you understand?"

I knew one thing, we had to get the hell out of there and go somewhere where we had a more controlled environment than here in this place. I really didn't know if we could find a place like that, but we had to try. "Toni we need to leave this place right now. We can either go to your place or mine and if that is not comfortable then we can go to the local library. Which do you want to do?"

We got up and headed to the cash register and I paid the bill and we went out to the parking lot. We walked to our cars, which were parked side by side and stopped in front of them. She looked at me. "Maybe we should just leave from here and go our own ways?"

That thought had crossed my mind, but I knew almost immediately that if we did one of us would never survive the day. "Toni we can't. If we separate, I have a bad feeling that one of us will never see tomorrow."

That seemed to get her attention and she started looking around. "You think they've found us?"

"I don't know, but I have this feeling that if we don't stay together either one or both of us will be in serious trouble in a short time." I could feel them watching us, but who the hell was them and was it a true feeling.

She had walked around and opened her car door and stood there looking at me. Her eyes were telling me that we had to do something and do it now. She then slammed the car door and walked around to my car. "You drive we can come back for my car later, now let's go, we don't have a lot of time left."

I was completely puzzled by this time but found myself opening my car and getting in as she got in on the passenger's side. We left the parking lot and she directed me to her place, which turned out to be a small house located not far from the restaurant. We pulled into the driveway got out and walked to the front door.

At the door she stopped and turned to me. "Darrel, I don't know what is going on here but I am sure right now we must stay together and figure this thing out. I don't mind telling you I'm really scared but I don't know what else to do or where else to go.

Chapter Six

COMES THE HUNTER

Toni unlocked the door and I pulled her aside and opened the door and stepped in. It was quiet inside the house and everything looked clean and neat. I stepped further into the front room and Toni came in behind me. We both stood there listening and looking when she finally started to say something.

I reached over and put my hand over her mouth and brought my index finger of my left hand up to my lips. She stopped immediately and I leaned over to her ear and told her we needed to look for any listening devices that may have been installed in her house.

Up till now I had never worried about anything like that but I guess my paranoia had started to kick up. Whatever it was, I knew that we needed to pay closer attention to our surroundings and take the precautions that needed to be taken. After all, the two of us had come together and I had this feeling that this had not been just a happenstance event, we were meant to come together.

I was no expert on sound devices but I knew enough to know that they could be hidden just about anywhere. Yet I also knew that the more secluded they were hidden the less sound they could pick up unless, that is, they were of such advanced technology that they could be placed just about anywhere and still receive a sharp and true sound pickup. The search had to be thorough and deep.

For the next fifteen minutes we looked everywhere we could think of and finally I hit pay dirt. It was hidden back of picture sitting on an end table and it was small and I almost missed it. Over the course of the next thirty minutes we found one in each of the five rooms in her house.

I took her into the kitchen and turned the water on and then pulled her close to me and whispered into her ear. "Get any documents you have about our situation, pack some clothes and let's get out of here. Keep it quiet and take your time we don't want to make a bunch of noise. May I suggest that we talk to one another and try and keep it away from our project? I think we may want to talk sex, what do you think?"

She leaned back and looked at me and started to giggle, I held my hand over her mouth. "No, just talk it."

Finally, she took a deep breath and started in. "Darrel do we have time to go to bed right now?"

Damn, she had to start out like that. She could have approached the subject some other way. So I responded. "Yes, we could if you want to but that would delay our getting to work on this stuff. Maybe we should hold off for a while."

She looked at me and smiled a broad smile and hunched her shoulders. "All right if that's what you want but I was kind of ready if you know what I mean."

I looked at her again and shook my fist. "Don't push it kid we have too much to get done and you're just trying to pull my chain."

"Right, I was just wondering maybe later, all right?"

I smiled at her and nodded my head and reached out with a pinching motion of my hand. "That's all right with me, now let's get to work."

We finished gathering all her paperwork and clothes and moved back to the front door and then left and locked the door behind us. We got to my car and pulled out. I drove for about fifteen minutes before finding a mall and pulling into the parking lot. We sat there a few minutes and then I turned to her. They probably have my place bugged as well so I think it would be best if I went home by myself and got my stuff and then met you somewhere.

After several seconds Toni turned toward me. "I think we need to find a place to stay right now and then we can go to your place and collect your things. I don't think we should split up; I think that as long as we're together we have a better chance of spotting any trouble before it's on top of us."

I felt myself nodding and then put the car in gear and pulled out of the lot. "I think we better leave your car where it's at for the time being, we'll pick it up tomorrow. Right now, I think you're right and so maybe we should head for El Centro and find a motel."

"I agree, and I know the perfect place for us to go." She replied.

It was only about seven miles from Seeley to El Centro. As we pulled into town Toni directed me to a place that was more like a resort than a motel, it was perfect. "Have you been here before?"

"No, but I've heard about it and felt that it was out of place for us, but the best place. It will probably cost us an arm and a leg."

I was sure this was the best location. "Look don't worry about that; I've got more than enough to cover any and all of our costs."

We pulled into the place, parked the car near the main entrance and I went in and registered us under a name other than our real non-actual names. I came out and we drove around to the back of the building and went to our room on the second floor overlooking the central pool area.

Up to that point we had seen no one that would have caused us to believe that they were connected to us or anyone trying to track or follow us. That did not mean they weren't out there, it just meant we had not seen anyone we felt was suspicious enough to be a problem.

I had gotten a two-bedroom suite with a small kitchenette. As we entered the suite Toni looked at me. "Why two bedrooms?" She had the little smile on her face again.

"Toni I'm not about to make an assumption that could place you in a difficult situation. No, the two bedrooms are the best way to go and even at that who said we had to use both of them?"

She started to say something, stopped and took her suitcase and went into the first bedroom overlooking the inner court and pool area and closed the door. I wasn't sure whether I had said something that was going to cause a problem, but she had been playing that bait game all day and I decided it was my turn. In time we would see.

The Gilgon unit had been tracking their targets across the country all along. The problem was they had lost contact with them almost as soon as they turned west from the east coast. Gaa wanted the two found and taken care of as soon as possible, but they were having a hard time following them. The man had been tagged and they were able to trace him to Black Mountain, North Carolina and then lost him. His car had been located, but there was no sign of him. A complete search of the area was carried out and once in Asheville the entire base unit got involved. He had gone right through the town where they had their main invasion base located.

To the south the units were working west in the lower states trying to locate the girl. They had not been able to tag her so they were working on her car and where it went. It was a slow tedious process, but one that would ultimately bring them to her and they could clear the slate and not have to worry about her.

Over the course of several weeks, they had tracked the girl and man to the southeastern region of the State of California, an area around the Salton Sea. As yet they had not actually located them, but they were closing in. The area of the hunt was fairly large, but they were onto their targets and it was only a matter of time before they would have them.

About thirty minutes later she came out of the bedroom. I told her we needed to head back to my place to get my paperwork and some clothes. I looked at her and saw that her eyes were red like she had been crying.

"What's wrong Toni? Did I say something to hurt your feelings?"

She looked at me and shrugged her shoulders. "No, I just started thinking about this whole mess and I feel overwhelmed right now. I don't know if we're doing the right thing or not. I know that before I was alone and now, I have someone to share this thing with. It's just that I'm not sure if you want me here or not."

"Toni we're in this together and I'm not about to throw you under the bus for my own safety. We're in this together and we'll leave it together one way or the other." I walked over to her and put my arms around her and held her close. She pressed in against me and hung on, that was my answer.

We smiled at each other and then I opened the door and we headed for the car. We drove the short distance to my apartment and both went into the building and up to my front door. Everything looked normal from the outside.

As I approached the door, I stepped up close to it and put my ear to the door. Yes, there was movement inside. I reached back and pushed Toni back down the hall and then as I turned away from the door, we quickly moved down the hall and headed out the front door. Once in the car I headed south from the apartment and turned west and headed for San Diego.

Finally, she asked. "What was it?"

"There was someone in the apartment moving around in there and I'm sure of it. At first, I thought it could be some maintenance person from the apartment building but I had no problems and there were no scheduled works to be done. I don't think whoever it was had planned on our returning at that time." I looked at my hands and they were shaking, damn that was close.

"Darrel, where are we going anyway," she asked as she was looking out the window and behind us?

I was doing the same thing, trying to make sure we did not have someone following us. I wanted to run west for a while and then head north and loop back to the resort in about forty-five minutes. "We're going to make a large loop. I want to make sure there is no sign of someone following us."

"What about your papers and stuff?" She asked.

I had been thinking about that and had decided that I would leave everything there and forget about it for now. If they were after the stuff then I had nothing to go back to, if not then it would be there waiting for me if and when I went back. I looked at Toni. "We'll leave everything there for the time being. I can reproduce just about everything from my head anyway."

Hunter had heard them coming and continued to set the apartment up so that when they finally did come to pick up his belonging it would all be ready. By then they will know that they have a benefactor working for them even if they have no idea who it is.

He watched as they headed out of the parking lot turning west and heading out of Seeley. He also saw the second car that fell in behind them shortly after their entry on to I-8. Hunter would need to follow and take some action when it was needed.

Toni and I then headed west on I-8 until we came to State Route 79 where we turned north heading toward Lake Henshaw driving through Julian. At the junction with State Route 76 we continued east on SR-79 to Warner Springs and then on northeast to

Aguanga where we got onto SR-371 and drove on to Palm Desert.

My forty-five minutes had turned into hours and I knew we would not get home that afternoon so we stopped in Palm Desert at a motel and spent the night. Yes, we took a room with a single bed and yes, we did get to know each other more intimately that night. It was probably the best single night I had had in my life. I hoped it was the same for her.

The next morning, we were up and out early and headed for El Centro. We then tied back into I-10 and headed south toward Mecca where we transferred onto SR-111 and drove down the east side of the Salton Sea and on back into El Centro. All in all, we had traveled more than three hundred miles after leaving my apartment before we returned to the resort the following day.

As we entered our apartment, she took my hand and turned me toward her. She put her arms around my neck and pulled me close to her and whispered in my ear. "That was the best short trip I have ever been on and last night was beyond anything I had anticipated." She stood there looking into my eyes and I guess she was either trying to think of what to say next or was waiting for me to respond.

Damn I was awkward when it came to trying to figure women out. I looked her in the eyes and decided to get honest. "I really do want to keep this relationship going. Last night was special beyond anything I have ever known. I hoped that you felt the same way."

I guess that was the right thing to say because next thing I know I had all the woman I could handle right at that moment. She gave me a big kiss and then skipped off to her room singing as she went. If I was reading her right, we were an item and she was ready to start working on the alien issue at hand.

I sat down and started going over the papers we had recovered from her house yesterday. I was impressed by the level of detail. It was clear she had a run in with some people that matched the description of those my friends and I had met in northwest New York State.

She was from Florida and had been in the Miami area with a couple of her girlfriends. They were there to spend the weekend. As she had related earlier, they had run into a young guy and that resulted in their spending the evening nightclubbing with him around the Miami area.

It was when they were leaving their last nightclub that the incident in the parking lot took place and she was running for her life. I was amazed she had managed to escape. It had been that close. She was a survivor and she knew she needed to put distance and time between her and the incident, and so west she came ending up here.

That was the strange part about this whole thing. Both of us had run from the threat against our lives and had ended up here. We both had seen the individuals that had carried out the attacks and were sure we were still being monitored but not approached. The question was WHY?

They, whoever they are, know we are here, that was proven by the sound bugs in Toni's house and someone moving around in my apartment. There had been five people we knew who died at the hands of men with three fingers at what appeared to be in the same time frame, except they were separated by fourteen hundred miles. That tells me there are more than just the five I saw in New York. So, from that I can be fairly certain these beings are spread out across the whole of the United States if not the whole world. That in itself gives me a feeling of helplessness.

Just then Toni came back into the room, walked over to the table and sat down across from me. She looked at the papers on the table and asked. "What do you think?"

I picked up the top page and held it out toward her. "I think this situation is much bigger and more complex than I first thought. Just between you and me there have been five people killed and we have seen no less than five or six of these three fingered individuals."

She was picking up a few pages. "Why don't you call them aliens?"

"Because, I don't know if they actually are aliens.

"Anyway, back to this information of yours. Do you have any idea as to why they would be after that man, you, and your friends in Miami that night? I mean did he say anything about being in trouble or did he say or yell anything when they finally found him? What about your friends, did they say anything that would indicate they were involved in anything odd or unusual?"

I could tell that my questions were causing her discomfort but I pressed on and pushed her for an answer. "Toni, there must be a reason why these three fingered people suddenly showed up and went after your friends and that man? You need to think, go back and search your memory for anything, even the smallest of facts that could tie things together."

As I watched her, she finally dropped both of her hands palm down on the table top. Her head settled back and she closed her eyes. I sat there waiting for her to compose herself and answer my question. Finally, she looked straight at me. "Darrel, to answer your question I will need to place a lot of trust in you and ask that you remain quiet until I'm finished. Is that all right with you?"

I was watching her and knew at that moment something vital and important was about to happen. "Toni, we need the truth, every bit of it. I will hear you out before asking questions or making any comments."

She nodded her head. "As I said before my girlfriends and I had gone to Miami for a weekend of fun. Yes, we had gone out that night, except we did not just run into that guy. I had met him about a week earlier in Tampa. We had stayed in contact by phone during the time between that meeting and when we met at the nightclub in Miami.

"There was nothing sinister about it. He was going to be in Miami, so we decided to meet at the club that evening. I didn't see anything wrong with his being there and my friends didn't seem to have a problem with it. It was all just an innocent meeting with no hidden agenda or anything like that. I liked him and he seemed to be interested in me.

"As I think about it, I remember it was strange the way we met. I was at the library doing some research on a company that was planning a new facility in Tampa. The city needed everything I could find on that company and so I went to work. I was a research consultant for the city and this was generally what I did.

"The particular area of research I was into was the location of the proposed facility placement. It was an open section of land that had not been used for anything for maybe thirty years and now a company was showing interest in that spot and it was something the city was more than a little interested in. Our main concern about the land was what had been there in the past and what, if any, hazardous issues were present.

"I was working at the microfiche machine when this guy walked up and asked

123

how long I would be. I had been there maybe an hour and had most of what I wanted and so I told him about ten minutes. He asked if he could sit down nearby and wait. I saw nothing wrong with that and said I didn't mind. It took me fifteen minutes to finish up.

"As I was picking my things up, he walked over to me and told me that he couldn't help but see that I was working on some research on the east side industrial park area and that he was there for the same reason. It bothered me in that I felt it was not an accident that he was there at the same time I was.

"I immediately asked him who he was representing, as I was placing all my research into my briefcase. He said he was there for the company that was considering the purchase and use of this particular section of land.

"All kinds of warning signals were going off by this time and I advised him I thought it best we not talk or meet now or in the future as long as we were representing our respective clients. He kind of looked like I had rebuffed him and seemed to withdraw. I started to leave and he reached out and took hold of my arm at the elbow and asked me if he could ask a question.

"This was not a good situation and I was ready to become real nasty. The look on his face was unusual and it struck me that one little question should not be a problem and besides I could simply refuse to answer it. I told him I would listen.

"His question had nothing to do about the research. He simply asked if it would be possible for the two of us to meet for dinner. That bothered me and I told him so. He then told me his name, Frank Benton and asked for mine. I told him and he continued.

"He told me that he would like to meet me on a non-job-related date and he was willing to keep things on the up and up and meet wherever and whenever I wished.

"Hell, I didn't know anything about this guy yet, so I proposed a meeting in Miami in a week and a half. I told him I would be there with a couple of my friends and if he wanted to meet with us, we could set a date and location, a mutual club we both knew about."

She stopped and looked right at my eyes. "Am I making any sense out of this?"

I sat looking at her and letting what she had said so far run through my mind. Why the hell would anyone set up a meeting like that with someone she had just met? That didn't seem right, it's not something I would do, but yet I'm not her and who knows what the hell some people will do. I shook my head. "Toni I'm having a hard time understanding why you set this date with this Frank guy in the first place. I mean, you had never met him before and had no idea who he actually was, and yet you set a date with this guy in Miami the next week. I'm trying to understand, but this is a little more than I expected."

Her mouth had dropped open by this time and she was realizing what she had told me was not just strange, but she didn't know why herself. She started to shake and then the tears started running. She was trying to grab onto the table top and regain control of herself. I wasn't sure as to whether she was angry or finally realizing what she had done.

As a result of that meeting three people died in a parking lot that night in Miami and she was fortunate enough to escape without any injuries. Yet when I think about it, and realize she had been the witness to the action of the same kind of people I had my run in with, I was wondering if her escape was all that fortunate after all. Is it possible she was meant to escape and head west and if so, just what the hell did that mean?

126

I reached out and placed my hands on the back of hers and sat there holding them. It was then it dawned on me that what had happened to her was not much different from my experience. I too had been able to escape and then it hit me. My friends had been targeted at the same time and why was I not then targeted. They let me go. Damn I hadn't seen that before. We had both been allowed to run and we ran to the same place.

As this realization hit me, I had started to squeeze Toni's hands and she was now trying to pull free. Darrel you're hurting my hands. That got me back to reality and I looked at both her hands as I held them and then brought the right one up and kissed it. I looked at her. "They know everything about us and our being here was planned all along. We ran but we ran from and to what they wanted. Do you understand?"

She sat there looking into my eyes and I could see the realization taking hold of her. As she became aware of what I had said and was connecting the dots her eyes grew bigger and bigger. I felt her hands shaking and knew right then and there she had no idea as to what was happening or what had been happening to her. She was clueless. Finally, she got her voice. "You're telling me, my running from that terrible incident in Miami all the way to here in El Centro was actually planned?"

By this time, I was nodding my head. "Yes, I'm afraid that is exactly what I'm telling you. Toni we are here because whoever they are wanted us here. Both of us, here in this place, at this time, and to top it off, I have no idea as to why this is happening to the two of us."

She pulled her hands away from me and raised them up in front of her with the palms facing me. "You can't be serious? If that's true then they could have killed us anytime they wanted to. There is a completely different reason why we are here and what we are supposed to be doing?"

"That's right. We have been played like a couple of puppets and they have us exactly where they wanted us all along." I was shaking my head in wonderment realizing we were clearly at the mercy of whoever these beings were and what they were up to.

Just then she asked a question that would open everything up for us. "How do we know it was those beings that have set this whole thing up?"

I had not expected that but when I think about it, I realized it would be rather odd for those who had killed our friends to then turn around and let us run free and guide us to this location. She was right, we don't really know if it was those beings or someone else who brought us here. The question is. "Who are the others who would bring us here?"

"Toni, let's take a look at this from a more controlled and orderly manner. Listen to me and correct me if I get off track.

"At almost the same time, the two of us where involved in a situation that cost the lives of a couple of our closest friends. Then, something caused us each to run, but we ran in a particular direction, west. The relationship between us was the actual assault on our friends, and that's when you and I headed west. But the important thing was we headed for the same location here in southern California.

"We both found the Superstition Mountains to the west of Seeley and have spent a lot of time driving out to and around that area. During this time, we both had the need to drive over to the other Superstitions in Arizona east of Apache Junction and spend time there. The end result was we returned here to Seeley, met out at the California Superstitions and here we are.

"In addition, our homes have both been entered and bugs have been planted.

"The most important thing of all was the fact we were brought together and I mean we were meant to meet and come together. For whatever reason, you and I were meant to meet. It's been our paranoia that has made us believe those who are tracking us were the individuals from New York and Miami, when in fact it is someone else.

"Someone who is involved in this situation, but as yet they do not want to make themselves known to us. I am beginning to believe we can relax, those who are tracking us are on our side and are not the subjects we are running from."

Hunter was sitting there with this wise smile on his face. They are truly unique beings and have the mental capabilities to go with it. That was a fine job of correlating all that has happened to the two of them and bringing all that information together. Yes, I have selected the right people to carry out what I need done.

Toni sat there looking at me. "I don't know if I can believe that right now Darrel.

We still have to be careful because we cannot say one hundred percent, they are not the ones we are running from. Darrel, we need to be careful and not jump into something we'll regret."

"I agree and it is for just that reason I feel we need to keep our location to ourselves until we are sure we have this thing figured."

I was sitting back watching her and thinking about the way we had met. For someone as fearful as she has been, I find it hard to understand how she could simply drive up to me as she did and strike up a conversation. It did not fit and I needed to dig into it deeper. There was something, but just what, was not registering yet.

Chapter Seven

THE SILENT BATTLE

Hunter was quietly moving around in the apartment checking out the paperwork his target had left out on his desk. He had finished setting up the Gilgon tracking bugs at target twos house and was now working in that direction in target one's place. He had been working these two targets all the way across the continent. Now he needed to monitor them continuously to insure they were not harmed or taken captive.

That was no small challenge for just one operative, but he had a reputation for doing the impossible and he was determined to maintain that reputation. While working this system up he had determined that two weeks earlier two hot opposition targets, Gilgons, were in the region and more were coming. That was his intent and it appeared to be working. As the number of Gilgons increased his need to maintain a close cover of the two targets was becoming his paramount concern.

These two targets were of the highest level of importance and any and all actions were warranted in this case. He had a total go ahead, and that meant he could use whatever force or resources he needed to, while overseeing the man and woman.

As the Gilgon search increased he would need to bring about more and more resources to deal with them. If it all worked out he would have them in just the right place at just the right time.

He had been there only a few minutes when he heard a sound at the door and moved off and away from the light and waited for someone to enter. There was a shuffle of feet and they were gone. He was sure there were at least two individuals there and both had left the area of the front door in a fast but quiet manner and that told him his visitors were his targets.

After a few seconds he moved over to the window and looked down, seeing the two of them leaving the building and getting into a car. For the time being he was sure they were all right and got back to work setting the apartment up for future monitoring. He had seen the other car fall in behind them as they pulled on to I-8, but they were not a threat yet, he had time.

By their actions he knew they had been anticipating someone in the apartment and he was sure they had been to target two's home and that meant he would have to go back and re-bug the place. This time he would make sure the tracking bugs were not findable even by the use of electronics. The fact that they found them told him that they were thinking and playing it smart.

He knew the targets were concerned about the bugs, because they had found them in target two's house. The fact was that the bugs were not there for the targets but for those that were pursuing them. Hunter wanted to know when and if the Gilgons had found the homes of the targets, which would mean that they were homing in on them.

He finished the process in the apartment and then left and moved back over to target two's house. He entered and found all the paperwork she had left in the place was now gone. That was all right with him, he didn't need any of that and frankly did not care about any of it. His job was protection and that's all he cared about. This was a special job and it meant he would be in the thick of things. No further monitoring was needed here. The Gilgons had found the targets as they left target one's apartment parking lot.

He had been at this work for eight periods and was well known for his ability to deal with the Gilgons. By their size one would think they were a formidable opponent, and if you were not paying attention they could well be. But, once you knew about them and their weaknesses, you could handle them quite effectively.

The average Gilgon was a big individual. Even among the women they were considered big averaging around six and a half feet tall and weighing in at around two hundred fifty pounds. Their general appearance, except for their size, was that of a normal human being except for a few differences, one of which was the fact that they had only three fingers and a thumb.

Though they looked formidable they were not that strong. As a matter of fact, the average earth male could fight and beat the average Gilgon. That's why they were seldom seen alone but almost always in pairs or more. When a man of earth saw one or two Gilgons just their size and appearance alone would cause them to avoid them, but if they knew the truth they could and would deal directly with them and in all probability beat them.

The problem was they, the Gilgons, had the numbers and the technology and that was his most threatening issue when dealing with them. So, when he moved against them, he did so with a ruthless attitude and showed it in the way he killed them. He left his mark each and every time and they have come to know him well and fear him. What he didn't know was that with the charge of these two targets he would not only be fighting for their lives, but his as well.

He was settling into the Hunter mode and once there he had a license to take any and all actions, he deemed necessary to carry out his duty. This Darrel and Toni would survive but what they would go through, if it did not kill them, would leave them scarred for life.

The time of the Hunter was on them and they had no choice in the coming events. What no one knew was that the world was about to enter into the greatest single war it had ever known. The only question was. Would it survive?

As he exited Toni's house, he noted the presence of another car just down the street from him. It was not a threat at this time but he knew they were onto his targets and that meant he had to step into a blocking mode and cover the targets movements from here on out.

As he drove off, the strange car fell in behind him. That meant they were after him. He knew another car had already left and was following his two targets. His next move was to eliminate the car behind him and then find the targets and take the unit following them out. The fight had started and he was in his realm.

As he moved along the highway west from Seeley, he watched the dark colored car following along behind at about a quarter of a mile. They never were good at tailing someone. They just seem to stand out and usually had not the slightest idea as to the fact they were. This one would be an easy take down. He just needed the right place and forty seconds to deal with them.

The right place came up less than five minutes later when he saw the junction of State Route 79 coming up. He knew that area well and also knew that his targets had taken that route. The tracker on their car had already told him that. When he got to 79, he turned and headed north taking the following car and its occupants off the main highway and into the more remote area he needed.

He drove around Lake Cuyamaca and continued on 79 until he reached Inspiration Point Road where he turned right and drove up to the lookout, parked his car, exited it and stepped off into the woods. He stood there in the shadows waiting and just as he expected the car came around the curve and pulled into the parking area.

They sat there several minutes, probably trying to determine what they wanted to do and then the passenger door opened and a large well-built man got out and stood there looking the hunter's car over. He pulled out his weapon and moved over behind the car and approached on the ready.

The first round came in on the driver of the dark car and hit him in the neck just above the shoulders. The round literally tore his throat out ripping his jugular vein in two and blowing his life fluids all over the interior of the car.

The man approaching the hunter's car swung around toward his car and the second round came in hitting him in the spine below the base of his skull. He was dead before he hit the ground. It was over just that fast and two more of them were out of the picture, no longer a problem.

He returned to his car and drove off watching behind him as the car burst into flames and the body lying on the ground did the same thing. That was why no one knew of their presence. When they die, they automatically cremate leaving nothing of their remains behind. Each death is final and each death leaves not a trace except in this case a completely burned-out car.

He needed to catch up with his targets and deal with the team following them. This time it would have to be a little more discreet so his targets would not be aware of the battle going on around them.

The battle? He had been at it for oh so long and there never seemed to be an end to it. The Gilgons had been trying hard to infiltrate this place and as yet had not been successful, mostly due to the Hunter's presence. There had been others like him but there was only one hunter alive and active at a time. He was the only one in this place, this medium sized planet located near a single star in the outer regions of the galaxy. Up until thirty-five periods ago he had never heard of this place, but why should he have. They had not tried to take this place before and so there was no reason for him to know of it or be concerned.

They, the Gilgons, had tried in other places and had been stopped. A few times they had been successful, but for the most part they failed the vast majority of the time. Yet they kept trying and kept coming, feeding the slaughter machine with their people in a never-ending drive to find, take and control other peoples of the universe. As far as the hunter was concerned it was a never-ending game and one, he rather liked, as a matter of fact.

How many had he killed during his time? A hundred thousand or ten hundred thousand he couldn't remember, he just killed them one, two and three or more at a time. They weren't that smart when it came to one-on-one fighting or for that matter a dozen to one fighting, he the Hunter always won, always.

He finally caught up with his targets and the car following them at Lake Riverside on SR 371. He settled back out of sight of the following Gilgons car and held his position. At the junction of SR 74 the target took a right and headed for Palm Desert where they pulled into and stayed at a local motel for the night. The Gilgons parked in a lot across from the motel and waited for their time to visit the targets. That time would never come.

It was three in the morning when the two Gilgons exited their car to head over to the motel. Neither one knew what was happening as the rounds came in hitting them both almost at the same time. Just a matter of seconds and it was quiet. A car slowly drove away from the motel area as two fires danced on either side of a dark colored car parked across from the motel.

The following morning the Hunter escorted his targets back to their chosen destination and then moved off into an overseeing position. There was nothing more for him to do at this time. It was not time for the final showdown with the Gilgons on this planet. That would have to wait until the right time and right place to be selected and then the purge would begin. He liked purges, they gave him a feeling of control and filled his spirit with the power of his domination over those he was to hunt and take.

The beings of this small place had no idea what was going on around them. If they did, they would lock their world door and never again venture beyond their own atmosphere. This planets history is full of the vile facts of war and battle. It permeates this place, yet they know nothing of the art of war and the art of battle when compared to that which exits beyond their world.

They are about to learn though, for when the purge starts there will be a killing field like none they have ever dreamed of. The Gilgons are many, but they are no match for the Hunter when the time is given and he must hunt.

That time is not yet and it is for this reason that the Hunter must tend to these targets to insure their welfare. No, it's not time and he must take each step as it comes to care for them, but his reward will be swift and dedicated when the purge starts.

As Darrel and Toni left the motel the following morning, they paid little attention to the police activity in the lot across from the motel. They figured that if the police were active in the area, then they would be safe from any problems that may come along. What they did not see was the car that pulled out of the market parking lot as they passed, falling in behind them as they headed back to El Centro.

As the Hunter tracked his targets, the normal process of dealing with the Gilgons was progressing. While he protected the one, the targets, he was putting together the whole of his organization plans for dealing with the Gilgons when the time of the Hunter came upon them. Till then he would deal with any additional soldiers that may or could be assigned to the targets in the El Centro area.

These two people had the evidence needed to blow the Gilgons cover and possibly bring the entire issue before the public and the world overall. The fact was, it made little or no difference, they, the Gilgons, would strike this world when they were ready and if that issue came early then that was all right with them as well.

The Hunter had worked hard to bring these two together and reduce his job of keeping track of the two of them. Once together his job was cut in half and he would be able to control events as he needed. He was aware of their attempts to research what they had seen and, in that process, they could create additional problems for him as time passed. Yet, it was the right thing to do and he determined they deserved that much, if nothing else.

Humans were strange beings in that they seemed to want to be in on anything and everything that draws their attention. They simply cannot leave things alone and have to know what is going on and stick their noses into everything. These two were no different, what they were doing could well cost them their lives and that is why he is there, to ensure it does not.

Several thousand periods ago the Universal Council came into being. Its primary purpose was to oversee things of mutual interest to all the participating parties that became a part of the Council. At that time, one society opted to go its own way and they were immediately seen as a danger to all civilized living beings. Those were the

Gilgons and they did not let the Council down.

During those early times they had attacked numerous occupied worlds and literally destroyed those living on those worlds, taking over all their resources and technologies. It was finally through Universal Council actions that the Gilgons were designated a predator society and a society that needed to be guarded against. It was even more important to assist and protect the young or defenseless worlds that had yet to reach the level of development the members of the Universal Council had reached.

Immediately upon that designation the battles started. The Gilgons were a large social structure and had reached out to many worlds and assimilated many resources and technology. For a time, the battle was a pitch battle with the outcome in question a good part of the next two hundred fifty periods.

At the end of that time the Universal Council achieved domination over the forces of the Gilgons and pushed them into a corner of the universe where they could be closely watched and dealt with. This did not defeat them; it simply stifled their ability to expand

and as a result their numbers reduced considerably during the ensuing time.

At that point, the battle turned into a conflict of subterfuge, subversion and stealth. It became a clandestine war with each battle taking place in the shadows and dark places of the Universe. It was because of this development that the Hunter came into being.

They were beings that were specially developed and trained in the art of shadow fighting. The art of mental manipulation and control and in that way, they controlled all that was taking place in the particular target area they are assigned to, their sole purpose being the engagement and destruction of the Gilgons.

Once a target was located the Hunter would then start his task, and one of the tasks he was charged with was to protect those who were the innocents in this process. Yet, that did not mean that all innocent was protected. As with any war there is collateral damage that cannot be avoided. The Hunter concentrates on those that become a part of the conflict as they come into or make contact with the Gilgons such as what happened to Darrel, Toni and their friends.

However, the fact that they were targeted by the Gilgons would become one of the central points in the Hunters searching out and destroying the Gilgon bases and units. In effect Darrel and Toni had become the bait in a battle that would soon envelop their lives and their fight to survive.

For them the issue would be who were the worst, the Gilgons or the Hunter? As both sides centered their actions on the two of them it would not be long before they knew who was their friend or benefactor and who their enemy was.

The problem was, neither side cared that much for their personal well-being, other than one side was there to control them and the other there to protect them. What would follow would be a swirling conflict of death and destruction as the two sides became more and more involved.

In short order the Gilgons would be using the two of them as shields as they try to avoid the hunter and keep the two targets between them and their predator. For the Gilgons it was a battle for survival and for the Hunter is was a battle of extermination and one that the two targets would witness up close and personal.

Chapter Eight

PREPARING FOR WAR

The third planet of the target star was considered a minor planet to the Gilgons and as a result their forces were well armed but small in number. It was felt that they would not need that many to overcome this planet. They had already developed a number of significant allies across the whole of the planet and it was felt that with their current level of control they would overcome the populace within ten years. They had four years left to go to reach their target, but now a Hunter has appeared and all was in jeopardy.

Allies, how odd it was that in worlds of this kind where the population has yet to reach a significant level of social development you could always find those within the population who would sell their soul and their world for financial gain. That was true even if they knew that what they were doing would be the destruction of their own world. Greed was a strange thing with people of worlds like this, it never seemed to change. There were always those willing to sell everything just for a time when they could be on top of everything or everyone else.

The Hunter was the worst news that could befall the Gilgons. Hunters were nearly impossible to kill and once they started there was little hope of carrying on with the current activities on the planet they were trying to occupy. Already there have been about half a dozen Gilgons killed by the Hunter and they knew that number would increase day by day.

That left them with one of two choices, the first was to abandon the planet and leave it for a later time, and the second was to take the Hunter on this time and kill him and finish their job here. The odds of doing either were questionable.

Gaa sat there listening to his command staff as they discussed their current situation and the presence of the Hunter here on this planet. One of his captains, Maa, was addressing the actions they had taken when it was discovered that three earth men had taken pictures of the execution of one of their traitors, Zdd, in upper northwestern New York State.

Maa continued "Maybe we should have left that situation alone and not made a big deal out of it. Even if they had reported the event and given the photos to the authorities, what would they have found? There was no body because it self-cremated soon after he had died. As he fell into the lake his body ignited and was ashes before it hit bottom and those ashes were then dissolved in the water of the lake. There was nothing, and as a result we moved too fast and took too many risks resulting in our current situation being discovered by the Hunter."

Gaa looked at Maa. "You know full well that we couldn't take a chance that this situation would not have resulted in a deeper probe by the earth authorities. No, I disagree, we needed to act and we still need to finish this so that no trace of us or that action remains. The same is true with the Florida event, which needs to be pursued and finished. Our task here on this planet cannot be completed until we are sure that our anonymity is ensured."

They all sat there and considered the two sides and then Kee leaned forward. "Commander what has already happened cannot be changed and will not change. Therefore, we have two choices of action. One is to pursue our current actions and kill the two earthlings and eliminate any possibility of their knowledge reaching their authorities.

"The other is to leave this place and let it die out here and now. I agree that it will still cause us problems later on, but they would not be insurmountable problems. Remember, these beings are highly skeptical of stories of space aliens and the likelihood they have killed people of this world. We've seen it time and again and we need to take advantage of that fact."

Gaa knew Kee, Gaa's second in command, well and valued his wisdom and skills in dealing with these Earth people. They were a strange lot and at times he had problems accepting the fact that these beings were not equal to his intellectual level. Kee kept that issue in check for him and made his task that much easier.

Finally, Gaa leaned forward and placed his hands on the table top. "We will pursue this issue to its end. We cannot afford to let even the slightest amount of information about us get out, even if we think these beings will simply brush it off.

"The fact is that there would be that little amount of fact that could get through and is the one thing that awakens this world then we would be faced with trying to change or control any number of actions that could follow. No, we will go after the man and woman and if need be, taking the Hunter out as well."

That was it, they had to be eliminated and it had to be as soon as possible. They knew the general area they were in and all they had to do is put enough resources into that area and they would find them in time. Gaa was convinced that was the path they needed to take and he set that down clear and to the point right then and there.

There was a feeling of unrest in the room as Gaa made his final decision, but he was the primary command on this planet and what he decided and directed was it, no further discussion would follow. Next, he turned to the command chart on the wall and addressed the forces at their disposal on this planet. "Kee, we have a total of three thousand fighters on this planet, is that right?"

Kee got up and walked to the chart and pointed out the primary locations of their personnel. "That's right, we have half our people located here in these United States and about five hundred in each of the areas of Europe, China, and Africa. In addition, we have fifty Challengers in those three areas and another one hundred in this country as well. That gives us two hundred fifty Challengers which is more than enough to take total air superiority of the world in less than a week."

Gaa and the other commanders sat there looking at the wall display when Gaa asked. "Is it advisable to go ahead and make our domination move at this time instead of the primary planned time?"

The others sat there looking around the table at one another. It was obvious that there was a lot of concern and uncertainty. Finally, the senior commander Lii stood up and walked around the table to the wall display. "I don't feel that we are that ready to move at this time. I have no fear of the world powers. They're an easy issue to deal with. My problem is the Hunter and his presence.

"You know as well as I and anyone else that his presence signals a major setback for us. We may be able to take control of this world right now, but when we do that, we must deal with the underground resistance of the world that will form as we move and then the attacks of the Hunter as he zeros in on us.

"Gaa, I'm not sure a direct move at this time would be to our best interest. I agree this is probably as good a time as any, but still the Hunter is our greatest problem. Gaa, my advice to you is to move easy and try not to take too much on at one time. I can assure you that taking on this world and the Hunter at the same time will never work."

Gaa sat there listening to Lii and feeling this was not the Lii he had come to know. He was being too cautious and appeared not to be too sure of himself, maybe he needs to be replaced. No, he's thinking and that is his primary value, he thinks things out and is always weighing the odds of success and failure. No, Gaa needed to pay attention to him and take his counsel into strong consideration.

Kee was sitting there shaking his head as Lii talked. He stood after Lii finished, showing the proper respect that Lii was due, and then addressed the command table. "Lii makes some good and reasonable conclusions, but I still feel we must move and move now. We need to be bold in this matter and if we put enough of our resource into the finding and killing of the Hunter then we will have this world in just a matter of hours. It's all sitting there waiting for us to successfully fulfill our primary objective and take a Hunter out at the same time."

The Gilgons were an authoritative society and when it came to their command structure there was little room for a democratic process. The decision as to what was to take place would not be put to a vote of the command table, it was Gaa's alone. He turned to the table and with one motion of his hand the eight around the table stood up and left the room and the decision to Gaa.

More than anything else Gaa knew that he had to keep control of his forces and not over extend his ability to carry out his prime objective. You do not fail a prime objective and still remain in a command position. You either accomplished it or you died trying, there was no other choice. His choice was the means by which he achieved that objective and this was his task, how to deal with the Hunter and still take this world.

He finally settled on a three-pronged plan. The first would be the elimination of the Hunter, which would be his prime target. Second the elimination of the two human targets, and the third the taking of this world, in that order.

His next problem was being able to do all three of the attacks without giving the world defenses a warning of the coming attack. It all had to be done undercover and discreetly. Yet, it also had to be foolproof and absolutely sure of succeeding. The two target persons and the taking over the world were not that big an issue, the issue was the Hunter, and that one point was what had him worried the most.

In the past, attempts had been made to take down a Hunter and each and every one of them had failed. Hunters were not pushovers. They knew what was going on around them every minute of every day and to be able to draw a Hunters attention away from any threat would be his greatest challenge.

It then came to him. A single strike to take out both the number one and number two parts of his plan would have to be done. Yes, that was it, we attack the two-earth people and draw the Hunter in and that will make him vulnerable to a direct attack.

Over the course of the next two days Gaa spent his time planning and building the system he would use to accomplish his target actions. He knew if he was successful, he would be a hero to his people and would be able to write his own future, once he returned to his home world. The stakes were huge and Gaa was entering into the biggest gamble of his life. He wanted the two-earth people and most of all he wanted the Hunter.

He had one caution enter his mind and that was what the Hunter was doing and planning. That was the biggest hole in his planning process. That meant that a lot of his planning had to take into account an unknown factor of what the Hunter was doing and planning. None-the-less he had to go ahead with his planning and implementation.

Meanwhile Darrel and Toni were still in their resort room, staying put until such time they felt the heat was off, and no one was coming for them. The Hunter on the other hand had ensured they were not being watched by the Gilgons.

His next move was to locate and scope out the Gilgons in this region. He could feel them and he knew that the race was on to take action. Either he took it or they would come after him and he preferred he take the initiative.

He returned to his stronghold and started to reach out and identify all those he was dealing with. Actually, his stronghold was not that formidable as far as structures go, but once the Hunter had settled in, he built a system of security that none could penetrate without exposing themselves to the Hunter. Within that place he would be able to determine all he needed to deal with, each and every issue at hand.

He started his search and reached out over the whole of the southwestern region. He found the two targets in their room at the resort and then started his mind scan of the whole region. It wasn't long before he found his first Gilgon target. He was a minor officer, but that was all he needed and he was ready to make the connection in order to build his knowledge of their current forces.

The Gilgon officer had no idea he had been entered and he knew nothing of the skills and powers of the Hunter. His commanding officers and the higher up of the Gilgon social structure did not provide that kind of information on their enemies. That information was power and he was not in a position to have that level of power in his hands.

The subtleness of the Hunters entrance left nothing for the officer to identify or even understand that he had been compromised. Unknowingly he would be the means by which the Hunter would learn all he needed to know for the coming series of events that would make the start of the war of the worlds in that part of the galaxy.

The mind of a Gilgon is a strange place to wander through. They are well organized and their mental makeup matches their social structure well. This one was clearly well organized and dedicated, yet he demonstrated inexperience and lack of understanding that reflected his youth.

He was the kind that would charge blindly into any situation and die without even knowing or understanding what the issue was that they were targeting. Absolutely not unusual for a Gilgon and in his case the perfect means for the Hunter to dig into the organization he was facing.

Having set up a tracking tag in the mind of the Gilgon he then set to work tying the Gilgons and the two targets together and working out their relationship. It would be the key to his understanding of what was happening between the two sides.

He knew the Gilgons were the predators and the two targets were the victims of the Gilgons plans. He also knew he was a major target of the Gilgon leadership as well. They would spend considerable resources to try and kill him. Unless he completely screwed up, that wouldn't happen.

Once everything was set up, the information started a continuous flow into his mind and he set to work tying all the data between the two issues together and preparing for the eventual conflict that was sure to come.

The key would be dealing with the Gilgons without the targets knowing what was going on until he was ready for them to know. They also had to complete the tasks that he was setting up for them. If all went right, this world would never know how close it came to total annihilation. Yet there would be a scar that would remind them of the dangers that lurk in the realm of space.

Chapter Nine

SEARCH OF THE PAST

Toni and I had settled into our hideout and were now getting into the job of going over the past several months of running and what took place during those times. It would prove to be a difficult process but one we needed to do now and not later. I still had that inner feeling we had been brought together, how I was not sure, but we had been brought together and it was for a reason.

I had yet to talk to Toni about that feeling and had determined I would wait until we had all the facts laid out and then decide when I would cover the issue. Due to our prior discussion, I think she had some idea as to what had happened to bring us together.

The key now was to go into everything we had on hand and through our memories and see what we came up with.

Though my apartment had been compromised I still had all the paperwork and pictures I carried with me wherever I went, and that included the pictures at the lake when we first met the three fingered men and witnessed the shooting. I never let those items out of my sight, they were my insurance and wherever and whenever those people catch up with me, I will need that protection.

The pictures, that reminded me of the lawyers and the envelopes I had left with them. I needed to make the calls and bring that issue down. I now felt that I did not need to see that the pictures were made available to the government and that I should retrieve the envelopes. I called the four attorneys and arranged for the envelopes with the safe deposit box keys to be mailed to me. With that done I needed to retrieve the envelope from the park.

I advised Toni that I would be gone for just a few minutes. The park was less than two blocks from us and I decided to run there and get the envelope and return. I felt that I was safe in doing that. The fact was that I was told it was safe, no that's not what I mean. I felt that I was safe. It took me fifteen minutes.

Once I had completed that task and got back to the apartment, we sat there looking over the rest of the papers and items we had. I then turned to Toni. "Toni, do you want to start or do you want me to?"

She looked up at me, and picked up a few papers off the table. "Would it be all right if you started? I'm not too sure just how to go about this whole thing."

Frankly I would have preferred she went first but that was not really important. I reached out and picked up the stack of pictures from the lake and started to lay them out. As I did, I told Toni the story as to how we came to be at the lake.

"As I said before Toni, I and my two buddies are photo buffs. It's our hobby to go out on photo taking trips and see what we can find and capture and bring back. We would take those photos and then build albums or other photo-based slide shows and see how well we did. A few have been sold and we did rather well with them.

"This trip was no different. We had spent several weeks planning the whole thing, selecting and locating the lake and the type of photo process we were going to use. In this case we had decided to do a series of panoramic shots of the lake which would take in around a hundred fifty to a hundred eight degrees of the lake view. It was a rather ambitious photo shoot.

"The plan called for all three of us to take a series of shots using our own independent equipment and then determine which series was the best for our overall project. Believe me when I tell you that one series of shots is difficult enough but when you're doing three sets at the same time, well that's just plain nuts.

"We finally worked things out so we could set up all three sets of cameras at the same time. We would stagger them one behind the other and offset to the right about three feet or so. When the first series of shots were done, all that had to be done was to move that camera behind the others and be ready for the second setup. Then the next camera would take its set of shots and move off and then the third.

"This meant each subsequent set of shots would be set back and off to one side from the other. It was felt that due to the size of the object being shot the offsets would not change the resulting series that much.

"We then went over the satellite pictures of the lake and selected a spot for setting up our cameras. We found a park on the southeastern side of the lake. Then we needed to select a focal point that all three cameras could focus on. We selected the end of the dock on the opposite side of the lake from where we would be working.

"We planned on a shoot on the first day we were at the lake, which was the Saturday of our trip. We had left home Friday after work and headed up to the lake and stayed at a motel in Plattsburgh, New York and then headed for the lake early Saturday morning to set up for the shoot. We planned three shoots that day, morning, noon, and evening. That way we could have three different lighting effects to choose from later on.

"We wanted the first shots with the light coming in from our right while facing the lake. The second shoot would be at high noon with the light overhead and coming in from just behind us. The last shots were with the light coming in from the west or our left side but while the sun was still high in the sky. It was all planned out and that was how it went up to that point, just as we had planned it.

"Ty had the first shot and then I was second and Jacob was third. We started the panoramic layout starting to our left and moving around and all the way to our right. With the camera set on a tripod all you had to do was rotate the camera and take each shot as you go. The key is to find a match point in the first shot and set it at the right of your view and then in the second shot, place that same match point on the left of your view and then continue to do that all the way around to the completion of your scan.

"We each did just that and when we finished all we had to do was change our film, place the cameras back in their original position and then wait till noon. We planned to leave our cameras sitting right where we had originally set them up. We would then be ready for the noon shoot.

"It was during our rest between shooting sessions that we had the visitors. As the car pulled into the parking lot, we all got up and walked over to our cameras and were standing there when the three men got out of the car.

"They walked up to us and I knew immediately they were there for one reason and it was us. The guy from the rear passenger's seat spoke and seemed to be the leader of the group. He stepped forward and advised us their boss had noted we had been taking pictures of the lake and he was sure we had gotten some shots of him. Their boss is camera shy and he wanted to buy all our film from us at a premium price.

"By this time Ty had stepped toward the man and was advising him we would not be selling our film and thanked them for the offer. The next thing I knew Ty was on the ground flat on his back. I didn't even see the punch thrown. All I knew was Ty was down and the leader was stepping toward Jacob.

Jacob raised his hands and reached in his case and pulled the roll of used film and held it out to the guy. He did the same from Ty's bag and then looked over at me. I had already pulled my roll out and was handing it toward them.

"By this time the other two had been stepping toward us and reaching under their jackets when they all froze in place. They were all looking past me and toward the end of the parking lot. I turned my head and saw a police car pulling into the lot. I turned back to the leader and he was smiling and gave me a salute, reached out and pinched my cheek then turned and walked off. As he walked by Jacob, he gave Jacob a pinch on the cheek as well. They left the area and we got Ty up and collected our gear and left for the motel. Our shoot was over."

I sat there looking at Toni. She was totally engrossed in my story and was a little startled when I stopped. "What happened after that?" she asked.

I continued. "At the motel we got my laptop out and I put my photo card in the card reader and we started reviewing the shots."

She held her hand up. "What photo card? And you first said that you waited till you got home before looking at the photos."

That stopped me in my tracks. She was right, that's what I had said before. The only question was why I had missed that the first time. "Well yes, I guess I forgot to tell you that when I gave the big guys the roll of film, I neglected to tell them I had a camera that held a photo card as well and so I kept it. And yes, I did forget the motel session with the laptop."

She was shaking her head. "Darrel that's what got you three in deeper isn't it?"

"Yeah, that was the one thing I did that you could call stupid." I felt my gut tighten up and tears starting to well up in my eyes. "I was hell bent on protecting all our hard work and never even considered this was more than just a shy millionaire wanting the photo film back. It never occurred to me there was something far more sinister taking place."

I got up and went to the refrigerator for a beer and then looked at her and held another up. She nodded and I returned to the table. I continued. "As we were scanning the film, I noted the boat in the water directly across the lake from us. From that distance there appeared to be nothing unusual about it. You could see there were people standing in the boat and that was about it.

"Then I zoomed in on the series of pictures starting from the first one and slowly moved to the right stopping and looking each picture over to see if anything was evident which sent those men after us." With that I started to flip through each of the pictures I had stacked on the table. I stopped when the stern of the boat came into view.

"It was just a boat, and a fair sized one at that, especially for the size of the lake. Anyway, we continued to view each picture until we saw, a man's body coming into view. I zoomed in some more so that we got the whole of his body from the railing of the boat up and then continued to scan to the right.

"As the left side of his head came into view, I noted a smudge on the picture just to the left of the man's head. My first thought was crap I got a blemish on the picture. I continued to scan until I came to the right side of the man's body and I stopped dead in my tracks. What we saw explained everything including the smudge on my picture. There was a gun to the man's head and between his head and the barrel of the gun was another smudged area.

"We sat there for the longest time looking at that picture of a man dying. I scanned further right and then the whole of the gun and a man's hand holding it came into view. That view would change everything for us. It was just a hand holding a gun, but there was a finger missing from the hand. The shooter only had three fingers.

"I scanned back to the victim and as I did, I let the view slide down to the rail and

170

we could see the victim's hands holding on to the rail. Both hands of our victim had three fingers as well. Toni, each one of us, as we recalled what we saw, had seen three fingers on every one of those guys, those on the boat and those who came to collect the film from us. At the time we hadn't seen or recognized that the three men who confronted us had three fingers on their hands. It was when we realized that the two on the boat had three fingers that it registered that the other did as well.

"Wait a minute. Now that I'm thinking about it there was something else that stood out and made an impression on me." A cold sweat started across my forehead and I felt my hand shaking. "It hasn't registered until just now, but I know this much it really happened."

"Darrel what are you talking about? I don't understand what you're trying to say?"

"Toni, I remember looking back out at the boat as those guys pulled up and something in the water caught my eye. Toni, the water was boiling. Not only that, there was a red coloration to the boiling water like there was a fire under water."

By now I was shaking all over and knew then I had seen something like that before. By that, I mean since I had started to run and it was there in Palm Desert as we were leaving the motel. I looked at Toni. "Do you remember when we left the motel in Palm Desert the police were across the street from the motel and there was a dark car there with two fires, one on either side of the car?"

She looked at me and started to shake her head no, and then she stopped. "Yes, I do remember that. I thought it strange there would be fires around a car like that, but I thought nothing else of it."

"Toni, I don't know how I know this, but those were the fires of two aliens being consumed." I looked at her and I knew without a doubt that I was right. "There had been two of them in that car and something had killed them both and when they die, they cremate automatically."

Panic seemed to flash across her face as she realized that I was right and knew I was right. Her face had paled and she was clearly shaking all over. "Darrel that means they know we're here" She was starting to stand up and look around the room. "We didn't get away from them, they knew where we were and they were waiting for us. That means they're here, right here at this resort and they are watching us."

I got up and walked around the table to her and she turned and buried her face in my chest. "No, Toni they don't and they're not here at the resort. It's something even more bizarre than that. There is someone out there killing these things and it is protecting us. I don't know how the hell I know that, but I do and I know it is true."

She looked up at me with a bewildered look in her eyes. She was shaking her head and trying to say something when it finally came out. "How do you know that? How can you be sure there is someone or something out there standing between us and those beings? What does this all mean?"

She was asking the same questions that were running through my mind at that moment. There was much more to this than we had ever imagined possible. It was not an issue of us against them. It was a trilogy of us against them with a third player unknown to us standing between us and those beings.

"Toni that changes everything, we are involved in something that is far beyond our own personal lives and it is going to get worse before it gets better. I have this feeling we need to stay put, no we must stay put and let this process work its way out. We are safe here for the time being and we must stay put until we are advised to move."

"Darrel, how do you know that? What is going on here anyway?"

She was looking me in the eyes and I could see she was not in a panic state now, she was serious and totally in control. "Darrel, we have become part of something neither of us understands or is capable of dealing with. I'm sure now we can no longer run and that staying here is the only choice we have. It scares the hell out of me, but I know now this is where we must stay."

Something, some process was present there with us, and guiding us at that moment. It wasn't like something was controlling us. No, it was far more complex than we had ever thought. It was more an advisor or something like that, who was watching out for us and knew far more about what was happening than we could ever determine on our own.

We were pawns in some game that was far beyond our imaginations and there was little if anything we could do about it other than ride it out and wait to see what came next.

Finally, it came to me. "All right let's sit down and get back to figuring this thing out. If we can't fight them, we can at least understand them or what is taking place.

"As I said before I had noticed a boiling in the water after the victim fell into the lake and from that I recalled the police across from the motel in Palm Desert and the two fires on either side of that car. It meant nothing to me at the time but now it fits and it clears up a lot.

"First of all, we now know that those beings have been following us. Second, we know we have a protector out there somewhere. Third, that protector is in contact with us in some way. The fourth thing is that those beings are out to kill us. I now know that these are all tied together. I am even more convinced we need, no we must, stay put right here for the time being."

I looked up at Toni and she was nodding. "I think you're right about that, we need to stay put and pay attention to what is coming to us and respond to those feelings. I also think we need to dig deeper into this, as deep as we can go."

175

We were being fed all this information in some way and I was sure we were just starting with this process. We had been talking about what had happened to us before we came out here when it hit me. Why had these things happened or these memories suddenly come together I have no idea, but it happened?

It was like getting a glass of ice-cold water in the face. "Toni it was him."

She turned and looked at me and tilted her head to the right while looking me in the eyes. "Him, what are you talking about?"

"Toni, it was the man who helped you in Florida and the truck driver that helped me in North Carolina. We both described him as around five feet ten inches tall and maybe two hundred pounds, right?" I was shaking by this time.

Her eyes lit up and you could see the connection take place. "You're right. It has to be him, but who the hell was he or is he?"

"I have no idea who or what he is, all I know is he was there when both of us needed help the most. We weren't escaping those people, because they were tracking us all along. He was running interference for us."

176

Just then the second revelation hit me. "It was the pinch that the alien gave us at the lake that caused us to be traceable. After that had happened, I started to crave and eat fruit like I have never done before. I have no idea how that works into this thing, but that explains why I had that craving."

Just then Toni threw her hands into the air and swung around toward me. "Damn I completely forgot. One of the men that got out of the car walked by me and reached out and pinched my cheek. I brushed it aside and just then all hell broke loose."

Everything was coming together and we were now getting a clear picture of what was happening. We still did not understand what all this was leading up to or what it was all about, but we knew there were some monstrous forces involved and we had better do as whomever or whatever was suggesting we do and do it now.

We both stood there looking at one another and then it came to me that I needed to return to my apartment right now and clear everything out of it and bring it all back here. I reached out and touched her hand. "Toni, I have to run to my apartment and get my things. I want you to stay here where you're safe and I'll be back shortly."

As she stood there looking at me. "Darrel, I don't think that's a good idea. I think we need to stay together." Then she stopped and placed her hands on the table top, looking down. "I understand what you're doing and I can go along with that. I'll wait here for two hours and if you don't come back in that time frame, I'm coming after you."

"Toni, you, all right? That was not what I expected you to say and it actually sounded a little confused."

She looked at me. "I know but something tells me it will be all right for you to go to the apartment. I don't know how, I just know."

There was something going on here that was way outside our experience and beliefs. Something, yes something was influencing us or trying to control us in some way, but I couldn't put a finger on it. I felt confident a trip to the apartment was safe, yet I still knew this was not of my own determination. I was responding to urges that I could not explain.

Finally, I decided to follow those urges. Besides, we needed that computer and all those documents I had accumulated. With that I gave Toni a kiss and headed out the short distance to Seeley and the recovery of my property. As I went to the door I turned and looked at Toni and she was standing there looking at me. We had made the connection and I knew that she was far more important in my life than I had imagined any one person could be. She smiled at me and I opened the door and headed out.

My trip to my apartment was uneventful and as far as I could tell I was not being followed nor did I see anything or anyone suspicious enough to draw my attention. I felt a heightened degree of awareness which again I couldn't explain. All I knew was that I was alert and driven toward this one target and that was my apartment. I reached the apartment and parked my car, looked around and got out.

As I walked up to the building, I noted nothing out of the ordinary. The same was true as I entered the hallway and started walking toward my apartment. At the door I stopped and listened carefully with my ear to the door. Nothing, so I inserted the key in the lock and taking firm hold of the key slowly turned the key and the door knob at the same time.

As I pushed the door open, I noted the living room was dark with no lights on. I reached in and turned the lights on and stepped inside. As I looked around, I could see the place had been gone through. Whoever did it did not care whether I knew they had been there or not.

Finally, my eyes settled on the dining room table and there sitting on the table in a neat pile were all my papers and next to them was my computer completely ready and packaged for moving. I froze where I stood waiting for something to happen. It was quiet and then that feeling came over me again, everything was all right and for me to get my things and clear out now.

I felt myself jump into motion and headed for the table. The first thing I grabbed was my papers and I headed for the door and down to the car. There was no one around and I got to the car and loaded my papers into the back seat. I returned back to the apartment for the computer and headed out with that and again got to the car and loaded the computer into the back seat.

All was going just fine and I knew I needed to make one more run to the apartment. My gut was tightening up and I found I was having a little problem breathing. I knew I had to move and set all that aside and headed back for the last load. It was then I noted the car pulling into the parking lot. The urge for me to continue came over me and I kept going.

I don't know what was happening nor did I know if that car meant any danger to me or not, I just followed the urge and headed for the last run to the apartment.

When I got into the apartment, I felt the need to close and lock the door and stand there and wait. It was quiet and I did as the urge told me and stood there for what seemed like an hour until finally the urge told me to get the rest of my things and move, which is exactly what I did.

As I came out the front door of the building, I saw the car sitting in the middle of the parking lot driveway with both the driver's door and passenger's door standing open. Just outside both doors and on the ground were two fires and I knew immediately that two more of the alien beings had just been killed, but by who and how? I had no idea; all I know was that I do as I'm told and get the hell out of there.

I shut that out of my mind and got in my car and left the lot heading back for the resort. An hour later I placed the last of the computer parts on the table in our room and then walked over and flopped down on the couch and laid my head back. Toni came over and sat down beside me, "You all right?"

"Yes, yes I am." I replied. "I ran into two more of those beings and the urge had me return to my apartment and wait and when I came out after being urged to leave, I saw a car stopped in the parking lot and two fires, one on the driver's and one on the passenger's side. It then urged me to leave and here I am. Toni, there is something, a being that is overseeing our safety and protection. I have no doubt of that now."

Toni sat there by me and laid her head on my shoulder saying nothing, just holding on. I guess we stayed there in that position for the next hour before I felt we needed to get going on our project. There was something to be learned in all that paperwork, and we needed to find it and figure out what it meant and where to go from here.

Toni stood up. "No, we're not going to do that. We are going to go into the kitchen and fix us something to eat and sit down and take the time to enjoy it and then once we have done that we can start working on the paperwork. But I am not going to let you work more than two hours, and then we go to bed."

I looked at her and I guess I had a look on my face that told her I was not too sure as to what she was suggesting. "Look I'm just a simple girl, but darn it I have feelings and wants from time to time, and I plan on filling those wants and feelings when they come up and it's time mister, there is no backing out of it."

She was right, and besides that, once she said it, I had those feelings as well. We set to work in the kitchen and put together a top-notch meal and sat down and enjoyed every bite of it. Finally, we had finished and we cleared the dishes away and set to work going over my paperwork. I knew there was something there. Something I had missed because of the panic I was in when running from the east coast to Seeley. It was important, but just what it was I could not tell. I hoped I would know it when I saw it.

This whole process had been running through my mind. Whatever it was, it was feeding the information that we needed to use a bit at a time. It was clear that we needed to know this stuff, but the fact that it was being fed to us in this manner bothered me. Why not have it all at once. It then came to me that too much too soon could be more than Toni or I could take. Besides we needed to understand all that was coming at us and when it came in short bits it made things that much easier. Yeah, this was the way to go and besides it was the smart way to go as well.

We never got any further. It started with her hand on the back of mine and I knew our days' work was over and it was time for play. Yes, I was ready for it and this time we would spend as much time as we wanted fulfilling her wants. Well, I had a few as well.

Chapter Ten

ALIEN CONFLICT

The Hunter had been watching his targets as they moved on toward their hideaway. From his stronghold he could split his mind and work on the necessities concerning the Gilgons and stay with the targets as they moved from place to place. His influence over them was well connected now and they were aware of his presence and were cooperating with him. He needed them to do their research so he could pull all they had in their papers and minds together with his intelligence and finalize his move against the Gilgon unit working this world.

He was also aware that the Gilgons knew he was there and they would do anything they could to eliminate the Hunter, at any cost. They knew they were at a disadvantage, but there had been times in the past when they had successfully put a Hunter down and achieved their planned goals. It would not work out that way this time.

Slowly he was building a plan for dealing with this unit. Slowly the targets were beginning to gain an understanding as to what was going on and how they fit into the overall picture. It would be the final step in gaining a total understanding of what has happened to them that will give the Hunter the last element he needed for his plan and ultimate attack. There would be loss of life on all sides as he initiated his attack, it could not be avoided. Collateral damage was common in these situations and this was no different.

Once engaged, not even the nation's military capability, located just a short distance away, will be able to do anything about it. They will try, but they will die as fast as they attempt to intervene in the battle as it develops. The Hunter had been in this type of a situation before, and always, when he left that planet, there would-be huge areas of the planet's surface left blackened from the battles that were fought there.

It was not desired but it was necessary. This world would have to sacrifice whether they knew what the sacrifice was for or not. The Hunter would carry out his objectives and would leave a trail of destruction and death for both the Gilgons and the people of this world to witness. The one thing that was clearly not going to happen was the death of either of the two targets, they had and will earn their survival, he would see to it.

The beings of this world were about to see and experience the use of weapons they had yet to even dream of on this planet. The power and magnitude of these weapons would bring to these beings the understanding they are not alone in this universe, and they are far from dominant as well. It would be a rough and difficult lesson to learn, but it would be one they would never forget.

This world needs to understand that there are others societies out in the galaxy. Some of those are dangerous, such as the Gilgons, and others, a majority of the known societies, are their protection. When a conflict develops between these two intergalactic forces this world will find that the terror and damage caused by the two sides is indistinguishable one from the other. A battle of this nature only takes into consideration the results between the two conflicting parties and does not take into account the damage done on a minor planet in an out-of-the-way part of the galaxy.

He would warn these beings and many would heed his warning, but more would reject it and those would die, to the last person. When it was all done those of this world would never forget. They would know the next time aliens came to battle on their planet, there is no avoiding becoming a part of the battle whether they want it or not. And there would be a next time.

Yes, he had seen it time and again and it always came out with the same results. There would be massive damage to the environment and beings that live in this region of the planet where the battle took place. There was little he could do about it. His primary obligation was to stop the Gilgons by whatever means he needed. In this case the size of the Gilgon contingent was small compared to other planets he had worked on and the extent of damage should not be that great. The problem was that the amount of damage would clearly destroy most of the southern quarter of the place they called

California and the better part of Arizona all the way to the Superstition Mountains.

In effect an area of about forty thousand square miles will be damaged. That would be an area inclusive from the Arizona Superstition Mountains to the California Superstition Mountains, about two hundred fifty miles, and from the Mexican border north for about one hundred fifty miles.

The heavily populated areas on the coast would be left undamaged which was his overall hope. When the time came, he would need to get the targets out of this area and to the protection of the Superstitions in Arizona so they could survive.

First, he had to draw the entirety of the Gilgons forces into this region and then isolate them here. That would be the most difficult part of his plan, yet he knew they would commit all they had for the opportunity to take one Hunter out, and that was his plan. He was going to give them a target they could never pass up. A target so important they would commit the whole of their planet-based forces to their attack.

He had been on site for only six months and had already determined the Gilgon forces on the planet were one of their invasion battalions of three thousand fighters and two hundred fifty of their Challenger air combat units. Considering the Gilgon's normal strategy, they would have evenly spread their forces out across the world and then concentrated another larger force in the one society on the planet that had the greatest power base and capabilities for fighting back. That meant this nation called the United States would have half of the Gilgon forces here and a majority of the Challengers as well. He would need to bring the rest on site before taking the final battle to them.

The Hunter had learned that the commander of the Gilgon contingency was none other than Gaa and he knew Gaa well. He knew Gaa for the cold-blooded personality he had. Collateral damage meant nothing to Gaa and the more there was the more gratified he became. Gaa had experienced a prior encounter with a Hunter and was one of the few who survived a direct involvement of that nature. Gaa would jump at the chance to get a Hunter, that was his personality and he would expend everything to do it.

The Hunter would as well commit everything he had to the task at hand and what he had was formidable. He, one being, was capable of total destruction of this planet in a matter of minutes. Where Gaa loaded up and carried all his weaponry to the site of the conflict the Hunter drew his weapons out of his mind and manifested them wherever he needed or directed them.

The magnitude of each weapons capability was all from his mind. Yet there were restrictions. Whatever he used must be contained on the planet where he was using it. That means he can destroy the planet to its last molecule, but he could not involve or impact any other planet or object in the rest of that particular planetary system, unless of course he could tie each location to the other.

That was his power, but the essence of his life force still had concern and compassion for all other living life forms and so he would keep the collateral damage to a minimum. There was no other way. Some would die or be injured and that was the cost of being spared control and domination under the Gilgons.

So, the process was started. The Gilgons knew he was there and they were starting to mobilize their forces. There was time, lots of time and so he now shifted his attention back to his targets. There was a lot to be done with them and he needed to get his targets working their next step.

Future meetings with the Gilgons would be helped by any and all additional information he could collect on their actions and methods. He needed to know if they had changed any of their methods and if so, just what had changed and when. So, he was dealing with the needs of the targets and his needs related to the Gilgons.

The most difficult part in dealing with Gilgons was the methods they used to target a planet. They would infiltrate that planet and prepare for the ultimate taking of the planet's resources and wealth. It was those tactics that he was most concerned with. Were they the same as before or have they changed tactics again? Whichever the case was he would need to know so that he could prepare his own plans and actions.

Over the millenniums their tactics have changed and have become more of a challenge when trying to find where their new victims were located and then getting there before it was too late. In addition, he had witnessed the growing levels of resistance they have been able to mount against him. Time and experience bring about change and it is that change he needed to determine and then adjust his actions accordingly.

Hunters were not perfect and they could and have been compromised in the past, but this Hunter was not the ordinary Hunter. No, he was special, a new breed that had been developed and sent to challenge the growing strength of the Gilgons. Being the first of his kind, the Gilgons had no knowledge of him other than he was a Hunter and they needed to deal with him.

Hunters are a combination of a biological being and machine, clearly more biological than machine. In the past Hunters were clearly recognized as just that, a being and machine, an android. But the new one was now indistinguishable from other beings. Their machine elements were now totally built into the being's body and have been fully absorbed into that biological mass.

One other thing, the definition of a machine included both their mechanical and their electronic components that went into the makeup of a Hunter. One would look at this mixed being as an android, yet the Hunter was more than an android. An android is a robot built and modified to appear as a living being while the Hunter is a living being modified through technology, with greater powers both in strength and mental capacities. This includes the infusion of mechanical and electronic components that are built outside the body and then infused into the body where needed.

The Hunter has a brain and heart and all the attributes of a living being. His blood is biological and flows through his body providing the nourishments the biological body needs to survive. Yet within that circulatory system there exists a system of nanomechanics and nanoelectronic elements that move throughout the body and carry out specific and general functions that give the Hunter the abilities he possesses.

Mechanically his system can build power bases throughout the body giving the Hunter strength beyond that of most biological beings across the galaxy. The system provides the level of power needed to overcome and no more. In other words, the Hunter cannot become so super powerful he becomes a power base unto himself. This building and transfer of power is an automatically controlled system so the Hunter need not concentrate on that issue as he deals with others matters and needs.

On the electronics side he has the processing power of a super computer, not of this earth but of the Universal Council, a system the likes of which the people of this planet had never seen and would not see for another five hundred years.

His nervous system was fully tied to the electronic system infused into his body. The expansion in his abilities to see, hear, feel, taste and smell had no comparison anywhere across the galaxy. His mental and processing capacity was enormous and was the reason for his ability to track and influence his targets.

It was through this ability to process that he controlled his weapons system. He controlled an extensive array of weapons all of which could be manifested at his will, either singular or multiples, whichever was needed at that moment.

His systems were continually monitoring his environment in all areas. The level of data being processed would make a supercomputer on this planet melt under the load. He was the epitome of advanced technology to the wildest dream or extreme. It was this being who would eventually determine the fate of this planet, this place they called Earth.

He considered this part of the galaxy as being the remote or frontier of the Universal Council System. It was an area just beginning the process of reaching out into space and learning the truth of its existence within the scope of the entire galaxy. They had a lot to learn and a lot of pain to go through over the coming centuries, but with any luck they would succeed and become a part of the system and continue to grow toward their potential and ultimate success.

It was not his job to assist them in achieving that goal. It was his job to keep the Gilgons from destroying any hope of them achieving that goal. Others would, in time, come and give them the assistance they would need to continue their growth out into the galaxy. But until then he must remove this thing that was there to end their progress and hope for the future.

If there was any gain for the world it would be in the witnessing of the power and technology that was being applied by both the Gilgons and this being, this Hunter. The people of earth were about to get a crash lesson in the power that exists outside this planetary system. They were going to learn that the scope of good and evil reached beyond their own planet and out into the space they were struggling to gain access to. They would come to learn that they were in no way prepared for that next step.

Chapter Eleven

PUTTING IT ALL TOGETHER

As he reached out for Darrel and Toni, he found both of them busy setting up Darrel's computer he had just brought back to their resort suite. These two had proven to be survivors and he felt assured they would be a benefit to his needs. The challenge now was to get them busy on the research he needed done by them and so he centered his mind on theirs and set to work.

I knew I had been assisted in the recovery of my documents and computer. I didn't know how, just that something or someone had been there to ensure my safety as I moved around the area collecting my stuff. As I pushed the power button to my computer I turned to Toni. "You know what?" I was looking right into her eyes at this point. "I have this feeling and I can't fully explain it to you, but as I went to my apartment, I had a distinct feeling I was not alone while I was there."

It occurred to me Toni had the most beautiful blue eyes I had ever seen. Why that feeling just then, I had no idea, but it was there. I continued. "As I entered the apartment, I could tell someone had been there but even more telling was the fact that the computer and my papers were ready for me to take. I mean it was all sitting there on the dining room table waiting for me. Whoever had been there left the place neat and ready for my return."

Toni was watching him moving around and setting things up on the desk, so once the computer was up and running, he was ready to start to work on their research. It wasn't anything in particular that caught her eyes. It was his overall demeanor and movements that drew her attention to him. "Darrel, what are we doing here anyway? Why don't we just pack up and leave this area and go someplace else far and away from here?"

She knew they were useless questions but felt she needed to say them anyway. There was deliberateness to Darrel's actions, almost as if he was being guided. It didn't bother her that much just that it was so precise and direct she felt something more than what they were doing was behind all this. "Darrel, this whole thing is starting to really bother me. It's like we were being directed or guided in what we are doing and where we are going, know what I mean?

I stopped for a moment and looked back at her and continued to set things up as I responded. "I know what you're saying honey, and right now I don't have an answer. All I know is that so far, something has seen to it we are safe and moving in the right direction. If something or someone is guiding us, he or they are doing a good job and we can probably be assured we are safe and will remain safe." I felt sure I was right and we were involved in something a lot bigger than we knew at that time.

The answer seemed to satisfy her and she went to work setting out her papers and laptop. Within an hour we were on the web and starting our research. I turned to her. "I think we need to look for two things. First, any reports of people who had been killed in odd and unexpected situations. Second, remains of bodies that have been found and were burned or cremated."

She turned to her laptop. "I'll go after those who may have been killed in odd situations." Then she turned back to me. "By odd, what do you think I should be looking for?"

I sat there a few seconds. "I'm not totally sure but my buddies were killed in one part of their apartments and then dragged into their bedrooms. The wounds were massive as well. In your friend's case, the man you met and your girlfriends, the assault happened in front of a huge crowd of people and it was fast and determined or meant to target and kill them and you. They missed getting you.

"Look let's do it this way. Find anything and everything that meets or matches the two situations we came from and then print them out. Don't try to make any determinations as to whether they fit or not, just print them out and that will give us the chance to go over each one in detail and make a decision on each one of them. I'll do the same for the cremation events. That way it should move things along a lot faster."

She nodded and started to work. It only took us a few minutes and we were starting to send articles to the printer and it was just minutes before we had a rather large pile of copies building up on the table. We both looked at one another as the pile built, we were shocked at the numbers we were finding and they all appeared to be matching up. A lot of people had lost their lives over the past couple of months and I had a feeling we were just starting to get into the overall numbers. We were in for a long night.

Three hours later we stopped and sat back and looked at the pile of papers. We had divided them into the two categories we had been searching under and had somewhere around fifty different articles in both categories. Toni stood up and headed for the kitchen while looking back at me. "Want something to eat?"

That drew my attention off the piles, "Sure, and a cup of coffee please." Dang, she looked good walking away from me, I thought. Now be a good boy and stick to the job at hand.

A few minutes later she returned with two plates with sandwiches on them and set them down on the table. She returned to the kitchen for the cups of coffee. Once everything was on the table she sat down and looked at me. "Well, where do we go from here?"

I picked up my sandwich and looked at her. "I guess we take one article from each pile and start reading in depth. I think we need to identify the location of the event, the number of people involved, time of day and any other detail related to the issue of our research."

I stopped, sat back, and again looked over at her. "No wait, I think we need to go over our own experiences again and in detail so that we have all the important information on those two situations down and ready for comparison against all these others."

We sat there waiting, for what I had no idea. "Know what? I think you're right on that, but I'm going to find it hard as hell to go over my situation again. Do you really think it will help?"

"Yeah, Toni I do, the more detail we pull back up the better the results overall." I paused a moment and thought about what she had just said. "I hate the idea of doing it myself, but I think it is necessary and will help in the long run." I could feel my face flushing up and a little knot forming in my gut.

We finished our sandwiches and Toni grabbed her note pad and pencil and started to write. "All right you first." She smiled at me with that impish smile she had and sat there waiting.

I pushed my plate aside and took the cup of coffee and settled down to delve into my situation. Though we had gone over our experiences several times before, I recognized that in each case our memory becomes clearer and more detailed. I don't know why, but I knew this was important and we needed to continue. As I said before, Ty and Jacob and I had been friends for many years, actually from our high school days. Over the course of those years, we had gotten into photography and not in a simple way. We had gotten into it in a big way and in time had purchased some of the best equipment money could buy.

Our normal method of planning a shoot was to work up a schedule of locations we wanted to hit over the next six to eight months. That was not as easy as you would have thought, but it was the opportunity to locate and find places that offered the best photo opportunities.

It was during this process that we came up with Lake Chazy. That part of the state told us that we needed to do our shoot there during the fall months when the colors would be at their highest degree of intensity. It all came together and before long we had ten weekends set up and scheduled. Did I say we all had weekends free?

Anyway, the time for Lake Chazy came and we did our usual thing, finding a map of the lake and deciding where we would do the shoot. With this lake it was a no brainer, we selected the park on the south side of the lake looking across at the boat launch. It was a no big deal plan, but it was a good one for the type of project we were working on, that being a panoramic photo shoot.

The weekend of the shoot was perfect both in weather and color schemes in the area of the lake. The Fall Season was right on schedule and there was a full spectrum of color with the trees still in full leaf. That morning everything went just right. We got to the location and set our equipment up and got ready for the right lighting and waited.

I remember the boat sitting on the water across the lake from us, just out from the boat launch. It was one of those low style cigar type boats about thirty feet long. I thought to myself that it was odd to see one of those on this lake. They were usually found on much larger bodies of water or out on the ocean. Other than that, there was nothing else going on out on the water or in the park.

Finally, the lighting got to the point where we wanted to start the shoot. Panorama shots are not easy and have to be set up correctly from the beginning. There is little or no room for error and when the shoot starts you must keep moving because the lighting is changing all the time.

We had set our cameras up one behind the other so that as one finished his swing, he could then pull the camera and move out of the way and the next could start his shoot. There was no time for messing around with the lens or adjusting the focus. That had to be done the first time and then the swing started. Each shot had to be at the right place to insure when we stitched the shots together there would be no gaps.

Ty had won the draw for the first swing and when he was ready, I started the count. He did his swing and then pulled his equipment and I started mine, when I was done Jacob came last. The whole thing took no more than two minutes total and we had three complete panorama scans of the lake. We had a total of three shoot scheduled for that day, the second at noon and the third at three or four that afternoon.

We wouldn't know what we had until we got back to the motel and had a chance to dump the shots onto the laptop and start our review of each of the three. If we did not like what we ended up with then we had a second shoot schedule for the following morning using the same schedule.

It should be noted that we use both film and data cards when shooting. The film gives us the old-fashioned means of reproducing our pictures and we loved the chance to work in the dark room on projects like this. The film would be placed in canisters and sealed for safe keeping while we worked with the data cards on our preliminary reviews.

We were in the process of putting our equipment back into position when the brown Cad pulled into the park and drove up to where we were. The guys that got out of the car, as I said before, were the biggest men I had ever seen. Damn, just to look at them was intimidating as hell. Ty and Jacob were clearly impressed as the three of them walked up to us.

The apparent leader started to talk, "You guys' professional photographers?"

Ty was standing the closest to the lead stranger. "No, we're just hobby junkies out on a photo shoot."

The lead guy turned to Ty and addressed him directly. "Well guys it appears that you may have taken a picture of our boss Mee and I have to advise you that our boss does not like having his picture taken, even by accident. So, he sent us over here to buy your film from you. It is our hope that you cooperate and turn the film over to us so we can be on our way."

Ty looked over at Jacob and me and then turned back to the leader. "Sorry sir, we had no intention of taking anyone's picture. Our whole purpose here was to get three sets of panoramic shots of the landscape and not people. I really doubt if there is any identifiable photo of your boss on our film." Ty looked back at me and then started to turn back to the big guy.

It was then that Ty went down so fast I didn't even see a punch thrown. First, he was standing and then he was on his back out cold.

The other two strangers just stood there. It was obvious they felt sure their leader could handle the three of us with ease and I was sure he could as well."

"Hold on a minute Darrel. Just now you said two things that were different from your prior recalls of that event."

"What did I say?"

"Darrel, you used the name 'Mee' and you said that Ty turned and looked at you before being hit." At the same time, she was pointing at her note pad. "You have never said either of those in the past, those are new."

She was right and I don't remember ever saying or thinking of those before either. Mee, who the hell was Mee, "Toni, I don't know where that came from, and the name Mee doesn't strike a thing in my mind. I used it as a name?"

She was nodding her head. "You said that the leader of the three said his boss 'Mee' did not like his photos taken even by accident. It had to be a name."

She continued. "Then you said that Ty had responded to the leader and then looked back at you and when he was turning back to the guy is when he went down. Darrel, you

209

were probably concentrating on Ty and never saw the blow. Ty was turning back to the guy and he would not have seen it coming either. Hell, it was a sucker punch."

I took her notes from her and sat there looking at them. "Toni, you spelled the boss' name 'Mee' why did you do that? How did you know that his name was spelled that way?"

She took the notes back and looked at them. "I don't know, I guess I just assumed it was spelled that way. What difference does it make anyway?"

"Right now, I'm not sure, but there is something about the way you spelled that name that means something to me. Right now, it's not coming so we'll leave that for the time being."

All right we've come up with two new things I had missed before, so let me continue with my recall and see if anything else comes up. The leader then pointed a finger at me. "Now I think you had better get your film out of those cameras and hand it over to us. I'm going to give you five hundred each for your film and call everything square, any arguments with that offer?"

Jacob's head was shaking before the leader finished the question and mine was not far behind. Ty still was not moving and I was sure he would not be for several more minutes. I knew he wasn't dead because I could see him breathing, but I still didn't want to experience the same thing.

We had the films out and in his hand in less than two minutes. He looked at them and then back at us and handed over three crisp new five hundred-dollar bills. I looked down at the bills, President William McKinley was on them, and immediately noticed that the leader only had three fingers on his hand. At first it did not hit me, but as he started to withdraw his hand, I noted the absence of one finger, the little finger.

I couldn't help myself I found I was looking to his other hand and sure enough there were three fingers. I then looked at the other two and they had their hands behind their backs. But when the leader turned and walked away, they both turned and I got a quick glimpse of both their hands and they too only had three fingers. What the hell was this all about and who are these people anyway?

I got up and walked across the living room and then turned back toward Toni. "It

211

never dawned on me that they could be aliens. I didn't even think or correlate that idea. God, I wish I had, maybe the other two would be alive today. All we could think of doing right then and there was getting Ty up and to the car and getting the hell out of there."

Now I was getting excited about this whole recall thing and it dawned on me that the name fit. "Toni that name, what was it? Mee, I have never heard of that name anywhere before. Frankly, it is alien as hell to me. What do you think?"

I could see the lights going on in her too. "Yes, I think I agree with you. We now know they are alien and the boss or leader of those three individuals was named Mee. I wonder?"

She was coming up with something and I felt it was important for her to continue. "Toni, don't stop. Go ahead and finish your thought."

She set her pen down and stood up. "That name means something to me, but up until now I don't think I ever thought of it, but I know that I heard it. It was just before the shooting started that one of the men getting out of the car called out to someone inside the car to let Mee know we got him."

I was stunned by what she had just said. The same name had come up in two places that were thirteen hundred miles apart. That meant that whatever kind of an organization this was it covered the whole of the east coast. I felt sick and knew we were really on to something and this thing was way more than we had ever thought it was or could ever be.

Toni sat back down. "Darrel, continue with your recall. We need to finish this. No wait, there is one other thing. You said that the leader put three five hundred-dollar bills in your hand. Before you said it was an envelope. Darrel, which was which, was it an envelope or five hundred-dollar bills?"

I moved back to the table and sat down and continued. "You're right I did say envelope before so where did the five hundred come from. No, it was an envelope and we opened it at the motel and I pulled out the three five hundred-dollar bills. I think I handed them out to the others and then pocketed mine, but I'm not sure of that now. Damn for the life of me I'm not sure just what happened there. Let's leave that right now and come back to it later.

Now where was I before, oh yes? Well, you know what happened after that. We went back to the motel where I pulled the photo card from my camera and put it in the laptop. Sure, as hell I had gotten a full one hundred eighty-degree scan of the lake and there was that boat. There was the shot of the man with the gun shooting the second man and both of them were three fingered.

We didn't wait for any further review. We got everything together and got the hell out of there and went home. I don't know how they figured we still had pictures of the shooting of the other man, but they must have because they came looking for us. If it hadn't been for Jacob calling me just before they came for him, I would never have gotten out of there.

I can still hear his voice screaming that they were aliens when the gun shot went off. From then on it was a panic and I eventually ended up here. That's it, that's all I remember about the whole thing, but yet I feel that there is something else, something I have missed but it's just not coming.

Toni sat there a few seconds looking off in to space when she turned to me. "Darrel, when you were talking to the leader of those three men you said the words 'our boss Mee'. Couldn't that be 'man' like 'boss man'?"

"No, it was 'boss Mee'. His speech was really good and clear and he said 'Mee' not man." I was sitting up and starting to stand as it dawned on me. "Damn its Toni, it was a name not a term. He said 'boss Mee' his bosses name is 'Mee' and I am sure of that."

"Darrel, what kind of name is Mee anyway? What language did that come from?" Toni was sitting there scribbling on her note pad as she was saying that. You know, one of those innocent moments when one is not really thinking but is mulling things over in their head. She stopped and looked at the pad and then looked up at me as her face went white and she started to shake. "Darrel, it is alien, isn't it?"

This whole thing was getting nuts and I knew as soon as she said it, she was right-on-the-money. But there was something else. As soon as she said alien, I knew I had heard this type of name before, but where? Where the hell had I heard something like this before. Mee, a capital letter with two of the same lower-case letters behind it, I had heard or seen that before and I needed to remember and remember it now. It was vital and I knew it was a big part of our answer. I also realized that the Mee name was the English interpretation of what their language name was.

It was overwhelming, that feeling I knew that name and someplace it was tied to. "Toni, I know that name. As sure as I'm sitting here, I know that name but I can't pull it up. I have heard it and not that long ago."

Toni looks at me.

I turned back to her and concentrated on her face.

"Now slow down and work your way back in time to that moment when you heard or saw that name. Take your time but work carefully." She was standing right in front of me by now and pressing up against me.

"It was when I was running. I had left New York State and was heading across North Carolina on I-40 to Black Mountain when I stopped. While there, I got a job with a guy who was delivering cargo and packages to that area and the next town Asheville, I think, or something like that. It was on one of the packages, that name was on one of the packages delivered at Black Mountain, North Carolina. But it wasn't Black Mountain it was Asheville and the name was Gaa and not

Mee." God everything was opening up now. But this time it was the fruit.

"Damn the fruit?"

"What fruit?" Toni asked.

I looked at her. "It was after we delivered that package to this Gaa that I began to have a craving for fruit, and I mean a craving. I still want the stuff, but it's not as bad as it once was."

She got this odd look on her face and started to back away from me and then put her hand to her mouth and turned and seemed to freeze right there. I walked up behind her and put my hands on her shoulders. "What is it, Toni? What did I say just now that caused you to react like this?"

I turned her and she looked up at me with her hand still over her mouth. She dropped her hand. "The guy we met in Miami was craving fruit and everywhere we went he would order up a plate of fruit. He was eating the stuff like his life depended on it."

"What was that? Say it again."

She stood there looking around the room and then back at me. "Darrel, that man I met in Miami had a graving for fruit. He was eating the stuff like there was nothing more important to him. We were joking with him as we walked across the parking lot when the car came into the lot and started shooting at us. The only thing that saved me was that I was the farthest away from the car as it drove up and I was able to duck for cover and run."

The realization of what she had said washed over me and I felt myself flush. The thought of me driving across the states and stopping time and again to buy and eat some fruit filled my mind. It was important. More than that it was life threatening important, the fruit was so important I knew it held one of the keys to this whole mess and I needed to determine what it meant.

"Toni have you ever had a fruit craving like the one you just described to me?"

She was shaking her head. "No never, I like fruit, but it was not like I had to have it. Even after that terrible night I have not had a craving for it."

She continued. "You said, your craving was not as bad as it was when you were coming out here. Are you saying that your carving for fruit is no longer there?"

"Well yes I guess so." My head was swimming and I was trying to understand what we were talking about. "No, I don't feel like I have to eat the stuff every minute of every day like it was then. No, I would say I don't have that craving any longer but I don't remember when the craving stopped."

By now she was pacing back and forth in the living room with her hand to her mouth when she raised her right hand. "Darrel, try to remember the last time you really needed fruit. The last time you went out of your way to buy some to eat."

I flopped down on the couch and laid my head back. "The last time that I can remember was." I couldn't. I couldn't remember the last time I ate fruit. That was nuts, I had to be able to do that but it wasn't coming. "Toni, I don't remember. For the life of me I can't think of the last time I ate fruit."

She came over and sat down beside me and took my hand. "Listen we need to back track our activities. Now over the past couple of weeks that I have been with you, you have not eaten any fruit. You have not even bought any. That means you stopped eating fruit before we met."

Then it hit me. "It was you." I sat up and looked at her and raised my hand to my forehead. "Toni, the last time I ate fruit was when I first met you. I was sitting in my car out near the Superstition Mountain, I was eating an apple, when you drove up and we started to talk. I put the apple down on the seat and I don't remember any fruit after that."

"I remember seeing you set something down and later on when I got in your car, I recall seeing a partially eaten apple on the floor board on my side of the car. Yes, I picked it up and threw it in a garbage can someplace, just where I don't remember."

I sat there a moment and then started to think out loud. "All right, I had developed a craving for fruit in Black Mountain, North Carolina. Prior to that I had no particular drive to eat the stuff, I ate the stuff but only once in a while and usually when berries were in season. It could have been because of our direct contact with the aliens, but if that was the cause then my two friends would have had the craving and I would have had it earlier.

No, wait my friends did have the craving for fruit. That was pointed out in the newspaper articles about their deaths. So that means that we all three developed that craving after the incident with the three strangers at the lake. That means that there was some means in that craving that gave them the ability to track us. Then how the hell did they not know where I was as I left New York?

No there is something else here that we're missing. It was something that happened in Black Mountain, something that I came in contact with that brought about a change in that craving. And the only thing that it could have been was that package we delivered to that Gaa in Black Mountain. No in Asheville."

Have you ever had a situation come up when you suddenly develop an insight, an epiphany? That moment, when everything came together and it all was clear, as if a veil had been lifted from in front of your eyes and you knew without a doubt that what just came to you was the truth? "Damn, the truck driver."

Toni seemed to realize just as fast that I had hit on something. "The truck driver, my God, it had to be that direct one on one contact with him. But how would that cause you to develop a craving for fruit? Especially when you already had the craving before you met him."

"I don't know, but it was him I'm sure of that. Something changed at that point and it had to do with the craving. Yet, I know he

221

was not one of them, he had all his fingers and he was smaller than me. There had to be something that happened during that short time together." My mind was spinning and I needed to stop and get things back under control and into perspective.

All right, I need to go back and start over with what took place and I need to start where I came into Black Mountain. Now I was pacing back and forth and Toni was sitting on the couch. "Toni, get your pad and start writing this down."

She walked over to the table, picked up her pad and pen, walked back to the couch and sat down. "Darrel, take your time and think this thing through. That will give me the time I need to write everything down as it comes to you."

I went back to that time and place and started tracing my actions. "I had gotten that far in my car and had decided to dump it. I ended up at a restaurant sitting at a table by myself. It was one of those places where there were booths, open tables and a counter with seats. I would say there were maybe fifty or so people in the place. It was not noisy, but there was a continual background sound of people talking and dishes being cleared or delivered.

"I remember I was sitting facing the counter and front door of the place. There was one man sitting at the counter and he was the driver I would eventually leave with after the job offer. Overall, there was nothing unique or out of the ordinary. I was just finishing my meal when the truck driver turned in his seat and looked right at me and then waved me over to the counter."

I stopped and reflected on his actions. Toni noted my hesitation. "What is it, Darrel? You need to speak out loud so I can get it down and hear what you're learning."

I nodded. "It's just that he turned to me and waved me over to him. Toni, he waved me over to him. He turned, looked right at me and waved me over. It was not an accidental meeting he was looking right at me. He was looking for me.

"I remember looking down at my plate and pushing several pieces of apple aside and picking up a piece of toast. My meal was almost all eaten. What was left were those pieces of apple, the pealing from half an orange, stems from some grapes and."

I have never heard a more silent room than I did at that moment. I don't think either of us was breathing nor had a heartbeat. It was so quiet it was loud as hell. "I had been eating fruit, a whole plate full.

"That guy was not one of the aliens, but he knew who I was and had set up that meeting, a meeting I knew nothing about. It was a time when we worked side by side and he never once questioned me as to where I came from or whatever. He just hired me to help deliver a number of packages and cargo and then he paid me off and we parted our ways. So, what the hell does that have to do with the mess we find ourselves in?"

I knew we were onto something but just what the hell it was escaped me. Toni was in the same situation. She was trying to tie everything together and not having much luck. All I could do was continue, "Look we need to concentrate on the driver and see what I can bring up on him. We spent almost nine hours together and there must be something that stands out and can give us a lead."

Toni picked her pad up. "Concentrate on the driver and give everything you can remember."

I started pacing again and let my mind slide back to that time and place. "As I said before, he was a little guy. No wait, that's not right. He was short but built like a brick. I would say he was around five feet six to ten inches in height and maybe two hundred pounds. He was all muscle and could move like a deer. I hadn't noticed that before but he was quick on his feet and limber as hell.

"He talked like he was well educated and his speech was clearly proper English. Come to think of it I never heard one slang word come out of his mouth. His speech was very clear and grammatically correct. Damn why didn't I notice that at the time. It was clear to me that he was way beyond the average truck driver.

"He never asked me a question but talked as if he knew everything about me. I mean when he talked it was with a matter-of-fact tone to his voice. Yet, we talked a lot and when I think about it, the conversation was centered on where I was headed and nothing about where I had been.

"We stopped for lunch in Asheville and while we were eating, he started to tell me about his job and all the strange people he had met over the years. Funny, it was then I noticed that he never looked at me. You know right in the eyes or face. He was always looking away or down at his plate. He had a plate full of fruit and was eating it like it was his last supper."

"Wait Darrel, you said a plate full of fruit. Darrel, you said the driver was eating a plate full of fruit and just before you met him you were eating a plate of fruit?"

It had gone right over my head, she was right, I said a plate full of fruit and then it really sunk in. That's where it came from, the driver; he had been eating the stuff like it was his last supper.

Toni had a smile across her face that lit up the whole place. "There you have it, the driver, now we need to talk about him, and what he looked like and how he was built."

I felt good, we had now traced the cause of the fruit and now I needed to start thinking about the driver. No wait it still doesn't match. I had the craving before I met the driver. What the hell anyway, it didn't match. No, yes it did, he had the craving for fruit also. He was eating the stuff for lunch and had been eating it for breakfast. Damn I was more confused now than I had been before we started this last recall session. What the hell was the link anyway?

I looked at Toni and she was just sitting there scribbling on the tablet and then she wrote the word 'LINK'. She looked up at me. "Darrel, it's a link between the three of you."

"What, what the hell are you talking about Toni, a link between the three of us?"

"Yes, a link between you, the three fingered beings and the driver. Darrel, in some fashion you are all three linked or tied together in some way. It's almost like being chained together or something like that."

God, she was right and now I knew what was going on. "Toni, the craving was the tie that kept the aliens tied to me so that they could track me to the Seeley area. The driver didn't want me to escape them he wanted me to lead them to this location. He used me as bait so that the three fingered beings would or could track me down. Toni, he used both of us as bait to bring all of us to this one place at this time."

Toni sat there nodding her head instead of responding negatively to what I had just said. "That explains everything. Now we really need to know everything we can bring up on that driver, whoever or whatever he was or is. Darrel what did he look like?"

What did he look like? I had already started to describe him before, but now I needed to get in to every detail about him. "All right Toni, I need to go over the driver's description again. As I said before he was around five feet six to ten inches tall and weighed about two hundred pounds.

"He was strong and had muscles that supported what I observed. I said he could move like a dear but I did not say that he had an air of self-confidence about him. He knew exactly what he was doing or could do and what it would take to do it. I mean he knew his physical capabilities well but even more he was mentally strong. No powerful. You could feel that power in his voice and movements.

"Now that I'm really thinking about him and focusing in on him, I think it was his mental capacity that really touched me. He knew everything that was going on around him all the time and that included me and what I was thinking and doing. I realize now as I worked and thought about how to pick up or move a package, he was right there telling me the right way and when to move and when not to.

"Another thing that registers now was the fact I felt comfortable and safe with him. I had been running scared for many hours trying to get away from the east coast. When I met him that fear went away and did not come back until I was on my own again heading west.

"There is something going on here and I'm still not sure just what the hell it is, but this guy was the opposite of the others I was running from. They were powerful and brutal. He was powerful both physically and mentally and at the same time pleasant and comforting to be with. What does that mean anyway?"

As I finished my description of him, Toni was sitting there and started to cry. What the hell anyway, why would she be crying? I moved over to her and put my arms around her. She was quivering all over. I mean there was not a part of her that was not shaking. "Toni, honey what is it? What did I say that hurt or scared you?"

She started to shake her head and reached up and touched my face. "You said nothing wrong Darrel. What you did was bring back a memory that I had not had for so long. The night of the shooting I remember running across the lot and off between two buildings. I knew they were coming after me and I was scared sick. I couldn't think.

"As I ran around a corner, I ran head long into this man. God why didn't I remember this before, this man reached down and lifted me up and then said I was to do exactly what he told me and I would be all right. He shoved me behind a garbage bin and then stood there waiting. About three minutes later the same car came down the alley and stopped by the garbage bin I was behind, one of the men inside asked this stranger if he had seen a woman run by there. The man simply said no and nothing else. The people in the car sat there looking at him and after several seconds they drove off.

"Darrel, the man that helped me was just as you described, and when he spoke it was perfect English. After those guys left, he took me by the arm and took me to his truck and drove me back to my car. He let me off and told me to leave town and head for the west coast. The description you gave matches him perfectly. Darrel, we both ran into the same man at a time when we needed help."

Toni stopped and seemed to freeze. She started nodding her head and looked at me. "He took me to my car. He didn't ask me where I was staying. He took me directly to my car. My girlfriends and I had been walking everywhere that night and had left our car at the motel. He knew where I was staying, and that my car was there. He took me to my motel and the parking lot and my car."

That revelation in itself was more shocking than all the other things we had been finding out. We had both met a benefactor and it was the same man. The question that came to my mind was why I had the fruit craving and Toni didn't? Maybe it was because of our gender, which would explain it.

No, it was the man friend she had come to Miami to meet. He had had a fruit craving and then he was found by the aliens and killed. Why didn't the stranger help that man? It was now obvious the stranger had some relationship with the friend of hers, and from that contact her friend had developed a fruit craving. Then he let the aliens kill that stranger and took Toni and saved her. What was the reasoning? Just what the hell kind of a game is he playing anyway?

Wait a minute, the friend of Toni's had the craving and he had to have gotten it from the aliens and not the stranger. He had no relation with the friend. It was with Toni all along and no one else.

It was like when we learned one thing, our memory opened up to another level of information or understanding. It then dawned on me, this person had helped us both, but what if he was still helping us. What if he was doing more than just helping, but protecting us as well? Where the hell did that come from?

Just then Toni looked over at me. "You know don't you. It came to me just now as well. He is still with us and he is protecting us from those others."

"The cremations, those where aliens just like the one that was killed on the boat. When he died, he burned, even in the water? This guy is killing those who threaten us and when they die, they burn." I knew I had it, and this thing was far bigger than I had even dared to consider.

Then the next revelation came in. I had the craving and it was from the aliens. Toni did not because she had not had any direct contact with the aliens like I did. That meant that the aliens were following me while she was running and leaving a trail for them to follow. The important and significant thing is that she ended up coming to me and I knew then and there that her coming to me was the plan all along.

I reached over and pulled Toni up to me and looked her in the eyes. "You know that he brought you to me on purpose, don't you?"

She stood there looking at me and slowly she started to nod. "Yeah, he did. It was all planned to go this way from the beginning. We were a part of his plan all along.

Chapter Twelve

SETTING THE WAR ZONE

Hunter sat there with a small smile on his lips as he monitored the two targets. They were close, real close and he was impressed. These beings are far more advanced mentally than he had figured, he thought. They still have a way to go, but given their skills and determination they'll have it within the next eight hours.

It hadn't taken much for him to influence their need to research their current situation and to find like events elsewhere across the nation. He just needed to make sure the Gilgons didn't interrupt their process. He set to work locating and monitoring those of the Gilgon contingent in the El Centro area. He didn't want to start killing the bulk of them off because it may draw too much attention at this time. No, he needed the targets to achieve their task and his job right now was to maintain their security and safety.

After the killing of the two Gilgons in the Palm Desert area, the Gilgon Command focused on that area and started to move additional units in. They had made the assumption that the Hunter and the two targets were in this particular area. The Gilgon Command was now committing their resources into the area, just as the Hunter had planned.

The Hunter had found a unit of four of their troopers still in that area following up on the prior two that had been killed across from the motel.

Yet he still had to deal with the two that were stalking one of his targets at the apartment a few hours ago. That was unavoidable, but there were no signs that those two had come up missing or were being searched for by the Gilgons. He would leave things as they were and deal with any changes as they happened.

He set up a haze alarm around the targets and then left for the Palm Desert area and a meeting with the Gilgon unit. His purpose was not a friendly meeting but one that would leave the Gilgon command reeling from the means and brutality in the elimination of this unit. In addition, it would confirm their belief that the targets were still there and solidify their movement into the area.

It was around eighty miles from El Centro to Palm Desert and it would take him about two hours to get there. He would then need to follow the unit around and determine the right place to carry out their elimination.

From a strategic perspective he was trying to draw the Gilgon command away from the El Centro area and concentrate their search on the Palm Desert area for the time being. When he wanted them to locate the targets, he would see that they did, but right now he was going to keep them out of sight and safe. He still had eight hours to go before it could all come to a head. They needed that eight hour and he was ready.

When in the true hunter mode all emotions die. There is no place for concern or consideration for the welfare of those he is tracking. Just as any hunter would do, he would set out to find, confine, define, and execute each and every one of them either all at once or one at a time.

Once in hunter mode they had no chance of surviving. It was a cold-blooded process with no remorse and no place for pleas of mercy. There is nothing, but nothing they can do to save themselves or each other. When initiated the Hunter has a known enemy and a known order to eliminate that enemy and he will never stop until that prime directive is met. The only other way out was the death of the Hunter and the odds of that happening were less than any mind could comprehend, especially with this particular hunter.

Yes, there had been hunters who had been killed, but in every case, it was more a case of pure dumb luck than anything else. Happenstance does happen and when it does it is a great loss to the Universal Council. The fact is only one hunter can exist at any given time, when one is lost it takes time to bring the next one on line and send them out. Much had been lost in the past during one of those mishaps. The only difference now was that this hunter had all the history of all other hunters in his mind and he could see and anticipate those events that could be of danger to him.

No, this one was as close to impossible to kill as any one being could ever be. No, this hunter had one prime command and that was to kill Gilgons any place any time and any way possible. That was all he did and all he cared about and he was a wonder at it.

They knew, they had seen his work and had heard of his invincibility, but they, the Gilgons, were programmed as well to carry out their directives and they would do that until the last one fell. That was the situation. It was a conflict that was going to happen and happen here right on this planet called Earth. Nothing could stop it and nothing could mitigate it. The collateral damage would be extensive, but the other choice facing the people of Earth was unthinkable.

He arrived in Palm Desert prior to noon. It was a bright warm day, a perfect day for the hunt. He knew where his prey was and he knew what they were doing. Now he needed to concentrate on the place, that location where he would confront them and deal with them. This one would be different, and it would be an event that the people of

Earth would never forget. It was time to start the process of bringing the battle to the forefront and let the people of this planet witness their salvation.

What was about to happen would bring the full alert of the national military in this place on Earth. He knew there were about twenty-one military bases in the area from Los Angeles south, and that a number of them had air combat capabilities both manned and unmanned.

Their alert would cause the Gilgons to move their air superiority units into the region and a short but violent battle would take place between this nation's military air unit and the Superiority units of the Gilgons. Needless to say, the Gilgons would come out on top and have complete control of the air over all of southern California and most of Arizona.

That would result in the Earth's military being fully mobilized and force the Gilgons to bring all their two hundred fifty Challenger air combat units into this area. With that the Gilgons would be forced to move their entire command into the region of the Salton Sea. He would have the whole of their power centralized.

He knew Gaa well and knew that he would take the initiative and once their presence had been made clear to the people of Earth, Gaa would attack and attack with vengeance. He would determine that once the situation had become clear to the people of Earth and their military, they the Gilgons, might just as well make their move.

In addition, they were prepared, and were frankly just waiting for the right time. The Hunter would give them the right time. The Hunter would give them the time and the place and a reason to attack and get this thing over with.

It wasn't hard to find the Gilgon unit. He found them cruising in the area of the motel where the targets had spent that night. The targets had holed up at a Comfort Inn at Varner Road and Washington Street. The Hunter had taken the two Gilgons that had been following them out in the parking lot across Washington Street from the motel. This was not the place he wanted to initiate the confrontation. No, he wanted a more public and more visible location such as a large publicly attended event.

As he scanned the activities in this area, he found that there were numerous retirement centers, the area was basically a retirement haven. There were few really large facilities available in the area except for golf courses and they did not give him the visibility he wanted for the next action. His mind then settled on the Indian Wells Tennis Garden.

This facility was more than just a tennis stadium, it held other events such as concerts and could seat up to sixteen thousand attendants. There was a concert scheduled for that coming weekend, Saturday evening to be exact, at the garden starting at four that afternoon. That would suit his needs just fine. Now he had to get the unit there, and that would be easy. He would give them the understanding that the targets would be there that afternoon in the main floor seating area.

He had almost forty-eight hours to set things up and carry out the public execution of the Gilgon unit. More than enough time to implement his plan, he had selected the perfect setting. He knew what he wanted to do and how he wanted to do it. This would be a demonstration that would leave the people of this planet in a complete state of shock and it would be the slap in the face of Gaa that he needed to get him to finally move.

That night a lone figure walked the main floor of the arena looking at the layout of the facility and determining exactly where he wanted to make his first appearance and where he wanted the Gilgons to be. He would be coming in his full battle dress and armament. There would be no question that what had just appeared was something more than just a stunt.

The Gilgons would be spread out on the main arena floor searching for the targets and he would have them cold. No place to run and no place to take cover. It would be then that he would give the world its first glimpse of intergalactic war and the magnitude of the power and weapons about to be released on their planet. The Gilgons would be sacrificed in front of the thousands present and the gauntlet will have been dropped at Gaa's feet.

Yes, there would be many natives of this planet who would die that afternoon, but compared to the magnitude of what was to come, the numbers lost on this day will be small. In time, they of this planet would come to realize the battle fought here was necessary in order to ensure their continued freedom and development. The alternative simply was not an option. They will pay dearly for their freedom these coming days but, in the end, they will find the rewards far beyond the cost in both life and natural resources.

Right now, he needed to check in on the two targets and determine where they were in reaching the results, he needed them to reach. If everything worked just right, they will have made the discovery and would be ready to set out to find the truth they needed to complete the task he had them working on. It made little difference if they actually were ready or not, their activities would continue even during the battles raging on around them.

As he entered their suite, he found the two of them huddled over the computer. Yes, they were close, oh so close. He reached out and gently instilled in their minds 'Superstition' and then pulled back and waited. It was only minutes before they both sat up and looked at one another and then looked back at the computer. The man turned to the woman and pointed at the Superstition Mountains in California and then dragged his hand across the monitor to the Superstitions in Arizona.

Hunter sat there waiting for the final piece to fall into place and then it did. Darrel stood up and almost ran across the room to his backpack and started digging. After a few seconds he came out with a notebook and started going through it. Here it comes, he's almost there.

He was almost jumping up and down when she went to him. "Darrel, what is it? What are you so excited about?"

He looked at her, set the notebook down and placed his hands on her shoulders. "Toni it's the explanation for everything that has been going on here and back east. It's so bizarre and unbelievable I can hardly say it, but here it goes.

"Toni the Superstitions are joined together. They are not singular or individual mountains located two hundred fifty miles apart. They are one and the same and one cannot exist without the other.

"There is going to be a great battle taking place here in this part of southern California and Arizona and the one place where we and others can survive this battle is on and in the Superstitions. They are like an ark where we can take refuge and still witness the battle that is coming, and it's coming soon. It will start this coming Saturday in the afternoon and so we have to get the hell out of here and get to one of those mountains.

"Not only do we have to go we have to alert as many people as we can to head for the Superstitions and take refuge there during this battle. Anyone not going to either one will surely die."

Toni was shaking her head in disbelief as he was explaining what was happening. It was then that the Hunter touched her mind and she knew that he was right and they had to move. "Darrel, who is that and why is he telling us these things, why is he trying to control us?"

By this time my mind was running wild with all kinds of thoughts and doubts as well. I looked at Toni and the look in her face told me that I had better get some control, or she's going to bug out on me. "Toni, I don't know who it is but it is someone who knows what is going on and I have a strong feeling that whoever it is has been watching over us and protecting us."

"You mean what is going on is being controlled by this person or whoever it is?" She was looking around the table top trying to find something. "Whatever it is, this thing has killed others in the process of seeing we were safe. That means he is still working in that way and if this is the case, we had better pay attention and get our act together?"

I didn't expect that from her. She was now thinking on a different plane than I had expected. The fear seemed to recede and, in its place, came a determination that spread across her face and set into her eyes. This woman was on track and we could now move.

It was speaking to us again and this time it was clearer. Each and every subsequent communication became clearer as they took place. We knew there was something in our paperwork that we needed to find. As we set the papers out on the table and placed them in their proper order we began to talk over our respective experiences.

I was holding a paper. "You know Toni we have identified the person who is assisting us. For me it was that truck driver that I worked for. The fact is he did not look anything like a super hero or an alien for that matter. Then you had that experience with that person during the shooting, as best as I can determine it was the same guy. What do you think?"

She seemed preoccupied but still managed to respond to my question. "I agree it was the same guy. The thing that bothers me the most is he seemed so cordial and helpful and then we find he is a cold-blooded killer as well. That bothers me a lot."

"I know what you mean, but that must be his nature or job being some kind of a body guard or fighter." I was still holding the paper and looking at it. "Don't you think?"

"Well yes, you're probably right. I don't know this whole thing is out of control and crazy."

I was holding that paper, looking at it, when it finally hit me. It was a page of notes written by Toni and they were relating an incident she had seen while exploring the greater El Centro area. I reached over and put my hand on her shoulder and turned her toward me.

"Hon, where did you write these notes?" I held the page up so that she could see it.

She took the page and started to read. "I did this when I was out at the Superstition Mountain about a week before I met you."

"Just where were you out there when you wrote it?"

She stood there for a few seconds. "Well, I was on the north side about the end of the road on that side, out where the ATV riders are always running." She sat back against the table. "There was a small parking lot there and I had stopped, facing the mountain, when I saw that light, I was writing about."

"You say here that the light was about half way up the mountain and appeared to be back into a ravine or cut in the side of the mountain, but you say nothing about size and color or intensity."

I handed the page to her and she started reading it. "Well, I guess I blew that but I can tell you now that it was a golden color. I mean that most lights are a variance of yellow to white but this was actually gold." She kept looking at the page and then stood up. "Wait the one thing that stood out and I failed to put it down here was that it looked more like a bubble than just a light.

"I mean it had definition to it. There were sides to it. God, why didn't I write all that down? Anyway, the light was nothing like any normal light you see. It looked more like a ball than an actual light and there was light inside it. Wait, that's it, there was light inside and it was a ball. I don't understand?"

I was looking at her as she tried to explain the situation and then watching the revelation of what she had seen wash over her face. I reached out and took her by the shoulders again and smiled at her. She stopped and looked at me. "Wait, Toni you weren't supposed to remember and know what you saw until now. Don't you see we're being fed each and every bit of information that is coming to us now? Whatever this being is, it is in direct contact with us and is working us into a system we must accept if we're going to survive.

"It has a purpose for the two of us and we must follow its directives. Right now, it has told us to prepare to move to the Superstitions and that both mountains here in California and over in Arizona are tied together and that is where people can go to survive what is happening or coming. How many survive depends on our ability to get the public informed. Do you understand?"

It was then that the Hunter gave them the final bit of information they needed. Toni was the one to receive it first. "Darrel, it's going to start in Palm Desert at a large tennis complex during a concert. The four alien sides will become involved in a fire fight right there in that location and a lot of people are going to witness it and a lot of people are going to die."

It then hit me and I turned from Toni and walked to the middle of the living room and looked up at the ceiling. "What is this all about? Why do people have to die in this situation? What is this all about anyway?" I found myself yelling at the ceiling and Toni standing there with her mouth wide open. I think I was going into melt down.

We stood there looking at each other not knowing just what to do next. I was sure we would get additional information and instructions, but I still could not understand or grasp what was happening.

Why was there going to be such a large number of lives lost. I felt the tears running down my cheeks and found myself in a near total state of helplessness. Toni walked over to me and laid her head against my chest and stood there while I put my arms around her. We were at a point where we knew what we were to do but did not know when.

There was something else that had to happen before we could finally move and start the process of trying to warn as many people as we could in whatever time period we had.

The fight was going to happen in Palm Desert in less than forty-eight hours, so that meant the time frame we were looking at was compressed and would require our moving and moving fast.

"All right Toni, here is what we're going to do." I had finally got control and took the initiative. "First of all, we need to get a few things together that we may need when we move. Second, we need to determine how we're going to start and do the warning to the public. That has to be a process we can carry out while we're running for it. The problem is that I don't have the slightest idea as to how to do that."

That was the frustrating part about this whole thing, not knowing how to carry that particular task out and still be able to warn a significant number of people between here and Phoenix, Arizona. It had to be a system that would reach everyone and give them ample warning to move and move now, but how the hell were we to do that. It was impossible.

Then it hit me, it wasn't supposed to be possible. It was a task we would never be able to complete. The only thing it will do is give the authorities the information that this thing was coming and they had been warned and if they don't take that warning to heart a lot of people were going to die. Why the hell was that anyway? Why would he send us on a task like that when there was no chance of our being successful in getting all those people to move? What the hell was going on here anyway?

"Unless, Darrel."

"Unless what, what are you thinking?"

"Darrel, this is just the first fight in the overall battle that is going to take place here. The information we give out now will give the people the time they need to head for safety and save their lives. It is not meant to save everyone, but to give a number of people the chance of surviving.

This being knows full well that once this thing starts the lives of all the people living in the area between the two mountain ranges are in jeopardy. This warning will give a good portion of those people time to get to safety and live."

I agreed with what she was saying and knew what was happening was meant to save as many as possible, but in reality, many thousands would die. I still didn't understand why this being wanted to do it this way. All I knew was it was going to happen and we needed to warn the public.

But how were we going to do that. We could call the media and tell them the story and that would probably result in a good laugh on their part and nothing in warning the people.

No that would not work and if this thing was only meant to save a portion of the people, then what else was there. I looked at Toni. "Look, there is something that is not going to work here and that is just calling the media."

She looked at me. "No, I don't think that is the way to do it. We have forty-eight hours before this fight starts and we need to get the media interested in the issue. They will not be just because of a phone call from us. But if we called the police at the time of the fight, and then informed the media, the response and actions of the police to the fight would generate the warning we were working to achieve."

She was right and I knew it, and then it came to me. "You've got it, and the being is letting me know that it is the right way to do the job. So, we need to plan on our moving out of here and to the mountain but he does not want us here, he wants us at the Arizona Mountains. We'll leave this afternoon and drive to Apache Junction and then do the calling from there. Once done, we'll move on to the Superstitions and find a place to set up.

Timing, it would all depend on the timing. We had to make the call to the police at the right time and follow that up to the media as well. Toni looked at me. "That's it. I know now we need to call the police about half way through the concert and then the media right after that.

The response of the police will draw the media in and then our call and warning will be foremost in their reporting of the events happening in Palm Desert."

This warning is not meant to give safety to or clear the people from that location, it is meant to inform the people of the battle that was actually taking place. The main battle will follow that one, and it will be big. It's going to be big enough to take out most of the Phoenix to El Centro area. It's not the Palm Desert area that is in total jeopardy, it's the total area from Palm Springs to Phoenix to El Centro and everything inside that area.

Chapter Thirteen

BATTLE IN THE GARDEN

We now knew that an area of around forty thousand square miles of southwestern California and southern Arizona was going to be engulfed in a battle between two alien forces and the number of humans in this area who would be killed would be considerable. The being who was watching over us had given us a task to notify the people of this region and advise them they could find a safe haven in the Superstition Mountains in California and Arizona.

We had forty-eight hours to notify the authorities and the media so that the public could be advised and then make a run for it. The only way possible was to advise the police of the fight in progress at the Gardens concert. That was to be followed by notifying the media of the same event and that police were on their way to that location.

But first we needed to get to Apache Junction and prepare to move into the Superstitions after making the calls. As we drove across the area between El Centro and Phoenix, we remained quiet for some time. My heart was heavy and I noticed tears in Toni's eyes.

There would be a lot of people dying in just a short time and there was nothing we could do about it. All we could do was try and get as many of those outside the concert to move to safety before the real conflict kicked into action.

It hadn't dawned on us that the being that was driving us had also placed a protective shell around us. We saw nothing and felt nothing and as we moved out of our suite and to our car, we saw no effect on anyone else.

Yet we knew there was something there just by the way we moved and the way our vision was affected. There was a slight visual effect that appeared as if we were looking through water. It was odd and rather worrisome. Yet it really did not impact our ability to move and drive.

Apache Junction was roughly two hundred thirty-five miles away and it was just after eight o'clock that morning. At four o'clock the concert would start and sometime during that concert the battle would start. We had eight hours to get to Apache Junction and prepare for the move to the Superstitions and then at the right time call the police and the media.

As we cleared El Centro we started to hear and feel something in the car. At first, I thought the car was starting to have a mechanical issue, but as we moved further east the sound became clearer and clearer. I looked over at Toni. "Do you hear something?"

She was sitting there looking straight ahead and did not move a muscle when I asked her that questions. There was nothing. I asked again. "Toni, can you hear something in the car?"

She slowly turned her head toward me and started to nod. "Yes, I can. It started out low and quiet and it is increasing in volume. It sounds like someone or something is talking to me. You hear it too?"

"Yeah, I do and it is getting louder." I was straining to try and hear it better and still keep the car under control. "What the hell is it?"

I started to slow down with the intent of pulling over when it really came through. "Do not stop. Keep your vehicle moving and go to Apache Junction."

Toni snapped around toward me, her mouth opens as if she was about to say something, but nothing would come out. I called out. "Who are you?"

There was a pause and then it came through clear as a bell and easy to hear and understand. "You need not know who I am or where I come from. All you need to know is that when you get to your destination you must perform your duties in a timely manner and without hesitations. If you desire as few casualties as possible in the coming battle you must do as I tell you without question. Otherwise, the number of dead of your world will be in the extreme."

"Then it has been you that has been guiding us the past few weeks as we came to this area and settled?"

There was a pause again and then. "You two were the sole survivors of a number of attacks on people of this world by the Gilgons. That made you special and it gave me the means of bringing this battle to this place. Understand that if I had not taken you into my care you both would have died way before this. There was and is a reason for that and I will now explain it to you."

We were both blown away by what was happening and somehow, I still managed to keep the car on the road. I looked at my odometer and noted that we had gone at least fifty miles and I didn't remember any of it. Yeah, it was protecting us all right. "What are you going to explain to us?"

There was another pause and then it started. For the next hour we would continue to travel across country to Phoenix and Apache Junction as the being explained what was going on. "First of all, I am the Hunter. I come from a society of beings that is well advanced over you by several million years. My duties are specific, and none revocable, and that is to protect other worlds from attacks by the Gilgons.

"The Gilgons are a society of predator beings that travel through space looking for and taking control of worlds that are not technologically advanced enough to protect themselves. Their purpose is to subjugate and strip those worlds of all their natural resources, eventually killing off the native beings. Your world has become their next target.

"For the last three of your years I have been tracking and preparing to deal with these beings before they started their take over and it is now time to deal with them. They will fight hard, and in the process will kill any and all beings of this world that they come in contact with. Their purpose it to create panic among your kind and hopefully cause me to either abort my attack on them or fail in carrying out my prime directive because of all the interference from you beings.

"That will not happen. However, their very own actions will draw all of their forces into this area and that will give me direct and total access to each and every one of them. That process will involve the use of weapons that have a massive impact on the planet and regions where they are used.

"It cannot help but kill a large number of native beings. To try and mitigate that impact I have developed two areas of refuge for your kind. That being the two mountain ranges you know as the Superstition

Mountains, one range located in your southeast California and the other in the southeast area of Arizona.

"A Haze Shield has been set up around both ranges and no weapon of the Gilgons will be able to penetrate it. As a second protection the shield has been set up to reject any and all Gilgons that try and gain access to the same mountain ranges.

"The key to your fellow beings avoiding death is for them to evacuate to the two ranges and stay there during the battle. In order for them to do that they must be informed of what is happening and where safety can be found. That is your purpose and job, to see that your fellow beings learn of what is taking place and where to go for safety. Once the battle coming up this afternoon has started, all beings in the area designated will have just thirty-two hours to get to safety. Any that fail to get to those locations will surely die.

"During the main battle there will be massive air battles between the Gilgons and your own air battle groups, but they will not be successful in defeating the Gilgons. They will be wiped out of the sky with little effort from the Gilgons. Once the Gilgons have air superiority they will attack the beings that have not taken your warning and many will die.

"During this time the Hunter will be annihilating the Gilgon battle units both on the ground and in the air. The actual battle will take sixty of your hours and at the end of that time there will not be a single Gilgons left. Nor will there be a future threat from them. They will never return to this planet.

"Now you know your duty and you will carry it out. Be warned, if you fail, the failure is yours. I have given you all that you need to achieve your goals, but if you fail, that failure will be yours and not this being. Do you understand?"

It became silent and the only sound was that of the car and the road noise it was making. I looked over at Toni and she was staring straight ahead. Her face was flushed and she was breathing hard. Finally, she turned her head toward me. "I think I want to go home now."

She was in shock and now I had to work her back to the present and get her with me and working on our job. "Toni, you know we can't go home now. If we try, we'll end up dead for sure."

Her lower lip was starting to quiver and she was shaking her head. "But I don't want to be here and I don't want to see what is happening. God I'm scared."

"I know honey but this is the way it is. If we run, those beings, those Gilgons will know and they will be on us faster than we could think and that would be the end."

I was watching her and trying to see if I was making any headway. "Besides there are a lot of people out there that are depending on you and me who really need us and need us now."

She laid her head back on the seat and sat there looking out the windshield. We travelled maybe ten miles before she finally looked over at me and smiled. "I guess you're right about that. We need to keep going but I'm so scared, I'm fearful I will fail you and all those people."

I reached over and put my hand on hers. "Look we are going to do this and do it right and then go to the refuge and prepare for whatever else there may be given to us to do, all right?"

She nodded her head. "I'm ready so let's do this thing."

It took us another hour and a half to get to Phoenix and then on over to Apache Junction. Once there we stopped at a motel on the east side of the town and moved into our room. Our job now was to set up our timing and the phone numbers of the police and several of the media outlets in the area. When we hit the time designated, we would have just minutes to contact the police and then the media and we would have to be direct and deliberate in those contacts.

It was now a waiting game and there was little left for us to do. Timing, it was all about timing now and if we did our jobs right, we could save a lot of people. I was still somewhat puzzled by the whole situation. Way back at the lake when my friends and I first met those men, I had no idea what the hell we were heading into.

When I saw the three fingers on their hands, I should have played the game straight and given them all the copies of the photos. Yet, as I thought about it, I realized that it would have ended the same way. They knew we had seen their hands and that meant we had to die. The only thing that saved us at that time was the Sheriff's Deputy that drove into the parking lot at the time.

It was obvious when we left that they followed us and knew where we went and who we were. The fact was they were going to kill us, and had only sent four men to do it, that gave me my out when Jacob called and warned me. At the time they were at both Jacob's and Ty's and were planning on me last.

For Toni it had been an even luckier situation. When they opened up on the man they were after, he was with Toni's girlfriends and Toni was on the other side and back from them by the cars. It was plain dumb luck that she did not get hit and was able to duck and run for it. She had help right then by the stranger who got her out of the area and to safety and sent her on her way to California.

Yeah, both of our survivals were a situation of luck and we were now here and the targets of the Gilgons wrath. All that has led us to this point and this place, and now we are the means of bringing them down and of drawing them, the Gilgons, into this battle with this Hunter being. In essence we are the spot in the middle of a target, the focal point for all this activity that will hit this area shortly. Scared? You damn well better believe we were.

We had no idea what the situation at the stadium was going to look like. All we knew was there was to be a fight and many people were going to die. This fight was vital because it would do two things. Draw the Gilgons in for the main battle and make the authorities and people aware of the fact this was not a joke or false report. In the end more would survive than would be lost.

Somehow this Hunter being had made it known to the Gilgons that Toni and I would be at the concert and that is where they would finish us off. They, the Gilgons, had been baited and we had been the bait. He had then, that is this Hunter being, sent us away from the area and set to move on to the cover of the Superstitions when the time came.

There was a degree of guilt we both felt being selected to be placed in a position where our safety and survival was almost guaranteed. Yet we were also grateful we would not have to be present during this battle and witness what was going to happen. I looked at my watch and we had one hour to go. We had safely made the run to Apache Junction and were in our motel room waiting for the moment to come when all hell was going to bust loose.

We had spent the past twenty-four hours working on our scripts and preparing ourselves for the series of calls we would be making. We knew the time element was critical in making the calls. As a result, the scripts where short and to the point, there was no messing around and no holes where the receiving party could interject or ask questions. We would call, they would answer, and we would read our script, nothing more and nothing less.

By this time over at the stadium people had been arriving for some time. The stadium was three quarters full and there were lines at the doors. It was thirty minutes till the lead band came on stage and another forty-five minutes before the main event started.

Among the crowds were four men dressed in dark suits with headsets on. They had entered the stadium as security personnel and in fact the gate attendants figured them to be security for the bands that were playing. They moved through the crowds as the crowds came in the gates and headed for their respective seating locations. The team moved on down to the main floor and set themselves up in the four corners of that floor to watch for their targets to arrive.

They would wait to hit the targets after the bands had started to play and the crowd was fully involved in the event. They cared nothing of the probability of collateral damage to those who were there. The targets were all that was important and anyone else meant nothing to them.

It was odd that they were trying to eliminate the two target witnesses and yet they were going to do it in front of thousands of witnesses. There was something going on here that did not make any sense at all. Why would the aliens make a move that was so public and so out in the open?

Why would Gaa permit such a move in the first place if it weren't for some other reason? Yes, they were after the targets, but they were also after the Hunter and knowing that made this move that much more understandable. Gaa had decided to make the major takeover move now.

As the lead band took the stage the team communicated that none had seen the targets and they must have entered the stadium without the team members seeing them. It was decided to start to walk the main floor and see if they could locate the two targets and once, they did the team would move in and finish the job.

Toni and I picked our phones up and started dialing. I called the police and when the dispatcher answered I did not give her the chance to ask questions I just read the statement to her and hung up. "This call is to warn you that there is going to be an attempted assassination at the concert in the Indian Wells Tennis Garden within the next thirty minutes. Don't ask any questions just dispatch emergency personnel to the scene. If you do not take this warning seriously then I deny any responsibility for those who will be injured and those who will die.

"There is a team of four men on the main floor of the stadium who will strike at their target and in the process will kill anyone and everyone standing in their way. My advice to you is to dispatch now and ask questions later."

With that I hung up and sat back. I was sure they would dispatch because of the number of like events that have happened over the course of the past three years, where people have gone on shooting rampages and killed dozens of people.

Toni had started to call the media and had made contact with her first target. "Police are responding to a gun fight at the Indian Wells Tennis Garden at this time. There are about to be a major battle between two opposing alien forces at that location. Your job is to notify the public to clear the area of the Gardens and to the public within the boundaries of Palm Springs to Apache Junction to El Centro and back to Palm Springs. Those who want to survive this battle must evacuate to either the Superstition Mountains west of El Centro or the Superstition Mountains east of Apache Junction. Anyone left in that area will die during the course of the battle that is building there."

She then hung up and called the next. At that point I joined in and started down the list that I had before me. It took us ten minutes to notify every media location and then we turned on the television to see if anything was happening.

It was less than thirty minutes later that the television news interrupted the program and reported an event was happening at the Indian Wells Tennis Garden. The report started out with the police being dispatched there for a reported gun shots situation. Just as they entered the parking area of the Garden it appears that the entire Garden stadium was engulfed in a huge fight of some kind.

A second call has gone out for additional police and other first responders. Information is sketchy at this time but it appears there have been casualties and more are being discovered. There is a direct report coming in from the field unit at this time.

"Jamie, a ship of unknown make or origin has just appeared flying over the parking lot and up and into the stadium. It has let loose an attack on the interior of the stadium and we can see some type of weapon being fired up and out of the stadium at the ship. It is turning into a massive number of weapons firing and raking the insides of the stadium.

"The din from the screams of the people inside is almost beyond belief. There is something of major importance taking place here and I'm not sure if there will be any survivors. We are trying to back out of the area and set up on a new location where we can see the stadium.

"There has just been a huge explosion to my right and one whole section of the

Garden stadium wall has been blown out. There are bodies being thrown everywhere. They are spilling out of the stadium in waves of death and destruction. Jamie, we're going to have to run for our lives in order to get clear of this killing zone. What in the name of God is happening anyway?"

"Paul, Jamie here, can you hear me?"

"Yes, Jamie we can."

"Paul, we have received reports that the situation involves two alien units fighting one another. Do you get that and understand what I just said?"

"Alien units, you have got to be kidding. I'll tell you this that ship that just came in is unlike anything I have ever seen. Jamie, it was a ball that was semi-transparent and gold in color. There was an occupant and it appeared to be human, well as human as we could tell. Do you have anything else coming in?"

"Paul, we have been in touch with other news outlets and they advise that they got the same information. With the warning of this event they state, and we confirm, that the person or persons who called told us, the people of this region, that area bounded by a line from Palm Springs to Apache Junction to

El Centro and back to Palm Springs need to evacuate the area and move to the Superstition Mountains in both California and Arizona.

"Those of us here feel that the information is bonafide and that we need to alert the public to evacuate and to do so now. All reports coming from the police are that their units have been knocked out and there are no survivors. Police outside the region are trying to organize traffic control coverage and set up a line of resistance to those carrying out the fight at the Garden."

It had worked and Toni and I immediately started to pack and move everything to our car. Our next job was to get to the Superstitions and hole up for the coming conflict. I had no idea as to where to go in the Superstitions', but felt that we would receive guidance when we needed it.

It was while we were entering the Superstitions that the first flight of alien air craft flew over us heading toward the battle going on around the Garden in Palm Desert. It was a formation of twenty ships moving northwest and at a high rate of speed. I had never seen anything like them or the speed that they were traveling. They passed over us and were out of sight in just seconds. The battle was building and there was little time for people to clear out. The Hunter being had told us there would be a thirty-hour period for people to move but, I was beginning to doubt that.

Chapter Fourteen

ARMAGEDDON

The Gilgon Strike Team had pulled into the parking lot in two vehicles and had parked at the back of the lot near the exit. They were fully armed and capable of handling anything that came against them. They had one task, and that was to locate the two individual targets and eliminate them. From all the facts they knew this was going to be a simple assignment. Find, control, and kill the targets and if others got in the way, then that was their problem.

Their second objective was the Hunter. The high command felt that the two targets were under the protection of the Hunter and if that were true then he would respond to the attack on the targets. It was the job of this strike team to engage the Hunter as well and if possible, kill him. There were no restrictions on their methods and means. This was a top priority assignment and Gaa expected full success.

As they approached the utility employee entrance at the back of the stadium, the sign up on the wall read Indian Wells Tennis Garden. Trr thought to himself, what's a 'Tennis' anyway? The Gilgon strike team made quick work of the stadium gate attendants as they passed through, locking the gate and hiding the bodies. They entered the stadium proper passing themselves off as security for the bands. In their suits and head gear they looked and acted like they were in their place.

They had brought their weapons to the utility employee gate in cases that appeared to be used for equipment by the bands. Once in the gate and in the entry tunnel to the stadium, they removed the weapons and slung them under their coats and headed for the main floor.

Each team member had a combination weapon capable of massive destructive power. With four units being used they could take on a fairly large earth based military unit and make quick and decisive work of them. Overkill, they cared not, they were after the targets and the Hunter and whatever they used to achieve their goals meant nothing to them.

The team moved down onto the main floor and took up positions near the floor entry points and started to watch for their targets. As the stadium filled the team became more aware of the fact that their targets had not come in or they had missed them. As the lead band came on stage and started their performance the team leader ordered his men to start walking the main floor and checking each row for their targets.

After another thirty minutes the team met in the area east of the first row and at the stage. It was then that they saw people pointing up above the band toward the top of the stadium. The four-man team ran out onto the floor area just east of the seating and turned and looked up.

It was a round semi-transparent gold ship hovering over the top of the stadium wall, over the area where there were no people seated. They knew immediately they were engaged and that their survival depended on their ability to lay fire on the Hunter ship.

They responded to the Hunter and his ship with full weapon fire. This was their most advantageous moment in trying to take the Hunter down. If they failed, well they couldn't fail.

Trr was the first to draw and fire at the ship. The rest of the team broke and scattered among the crowds of people and started firing on the ship as well. People were starting to break and run or dive for the floor when the ship cut loose with a palisade of fire that literally raked the main floor of the stadium.

By this time the Gilgons had upped their weapons level and were raking the whole of the upper area of the stadium hitting the ship with everything they had but it was to no avail. The Hunter was targeting in on them and their situation was hopeless, yet they kept on fighting.

Around them the people were falling like wheat before the cutters. Besides the Hunter ship the Gilgons had gone to firing into the crowds that were trying to run and cutting them down by the hundreds. If the targets were in there, they were going to get them if it was the last thing they did.

The intensity of fire between the Gilgons and the Hunter ship was increasing moment by moment. Whole sections of the stadium were being hit and crumpling under the concentrated fire that was hitting the structure. People literally spilled out of the stadium onto the parking lot in a mad mixture of concrete, seating, flooring materials and bodies.

Up to that point the Gilgon unit had been holding its own. Their body armor was doing its job and they were taking the Hunters weapons well. One would think that it was a standoff and the ones really paying for all the shooting were the people who were now running for their lives.

Finally, the Hunter put his ship into full on attack and raked the entirety of the stadium killing the remaining members of the Gilgon unit, their battle armor could not resist the power of the Hunters weapons. Thousands of the concert attendees were still trying to get out of the stadium and away from the battle that was raging around them. Between the two forces there was little or no concern for these lowly creatures that inhabited this planet. What was important was the winning of the conflict that was building and building fast.

The Hunter knew what was taking place was an absolute necessity. He knew the governing body of these beings would never believe what was coming at them and so he had to give them a demonstration. Something that would get their attention like nothing else they could ever dream of. A lot of their beings were going to die that day, but this was the way to make them understand there was far more going on here than they could ever conceive or understand without a demonstration.

He had caught them cold and knew they had no chance at all of coming out of this trap alive. So, they did what he knew they would do. They turned their weapons on these beings in hopes the Hunter would pull back first, and second, they would still find and kill the two targets they were after. The battle only lasted a short time, maybe ten or fifteen minutes but he had done all he had planned. The message had been sent and the people of this world knew without a doubt that aliens were real, and most of all, they were right there on their planet and in their faces.

Next, he had drawn Gaa out and now the real battle would take place. There was time for the people of this world to clear the battle zone. They had thirty hours to do that. Yes, the Gilgons had air superiority crafts coming into the area right now, but they would not engage the Hunter until they had cleared the air of any Earth based forces.

The Hunter had set the boundaries of the battle zone and the Gilgons were now claiming air superiority in that zone. Upon the arrival of the Gilgon air ships the people of this nation launched their own offensive against them. The Hunter was impressed with the numbers and types of aircraft the beings of this planet put into the air against the Gilgons. Not only that, but they were highly advanced in their ability to maneuver and operate their aircraft.

The air unit out of the base just north of the City of Seeley demonstrated an advanced capability and in fact gave the Gilgons more than they had anticipated. A number of Gilgon air superiority ships were taken out by that unit before they were finally neutralized.

It would take the Gilgons thirty hours to gain air superiority over the area of the coming battle. The majority of that time would be spent trying to overcome and defeat the air unit from the base north of Seeley.

The first Gilgon ships to enter the battle were the ships that were assigned to the United States. They numbered one hundred and when they came into the battle zone, they were faced with several hundred earth-based fighting units. It was almost an overwhelming engagement and the Gilgons lost a number of ships during that early period of the battle. But once their other ships from the other world bases started to arrive the battle began to swing in favor of the Gilgons.

The Earth ships fought well, giving as much as they were taking. This was something new to the Hunter, seeing one of the planet-based systems attack, hold their own and knock down a number of the Gilgon ships. He had never seen this before. This one special unit the Earth beings sent into combat was almost more than the Gilgon could handle.

That unit consisted of just ten or fifteen ships but they were probably a match for any Gilgon pilot out there. They gave the Gilgons a real run for their money. That was directly responsible for giving the people in the battle area time to evacuate to the Superstitions.

While the air battle raged the media in the area informed the people where to go and why they needed to go there. They had thirty hours to evacuate and then the probability of their being killed was one hundred percent.

The reality of what happening had hit home fast and clear and the people knew that and they responded.

Toni and I were in our position in the Superstitions and we saw the line of vehicles heading toward the mountains. It was unbelievable. The skies were full of aircraft of every kind and shape and they were fully engaged in battle. We knew that a lot of our military people were giving everything they had to give in order that those trying to evacuate the region at least had a chance of making it. They fought like people possessed. Some survived but most lost their lives as they were overcome by the numbers of Gilgon craft. But they did it, they drew them in and now all the combat and support elements of the Gilgon forces were present and ready for the final battle.

We could see the progression of the air battle as the Gilgon units slowly overcame the defense units. The ferocity of the attack by the defending Earth units had taken them by surprise. They had not expected that level of resistance and the numbers that were thrown at them. For fifteen hours the battle had raged and we could not tell who was winning.

After that we could see the numbers of defenders falling off as the Gilgons gained air superiority. They did not appear to be interested in the people evacuating the region but instead appeared to be concentrating on their own recovery and preparations for the coming engagement with the Hunter.

The masses of people from the region moved out and into the two Superstition Mountain ranges. Local rangers and law enforcement were present to help the people move into the mountains or park their cars and then walk into the mountains.

We hadn't realized that the Hunter had actually put a shield over the mountains until just a short time before the actual major battle when a Gilgon ship came in on the Arizona range and tried to shoot into the people that had taken refuge in the mountains. The ships weapons were unable to penetrate the shield and once they realized that they never tried to hit us again.

It all started at eleven o'clock that evening after the thirty hours had passed. The Gilgons had taken full control of the area and had consolidated their position and were preparing for a counterattack by the world forces. The problem was those forces never came. All the military capabilities of the nation had been neutralized somehow and now the Gilgons had an unopposed access to the most powerful nation on this planet except for one thing, and that was coming right at them at exactly eleven o'clock that evening.

At first, they only saw a pin point of light coming in from the north. It was moving fast and had an intensity that overwhelmed any other light source either in the sky or on the ground. Then the unexpected happened and the war was on.

The entire region consisting of the area between Palm Springs to Phoenix to El Centro back to Palm Springs was closed down trapping the Gilgon forces within that area. Any attempt by their air superiority craft to go outside that regional boundary resulted in the total destruction of the aircraft when it hit the boundary.

The Hunter had his prey trapped in the area and he would now start the extermination of the entire force. It would be a night of carnage as he systematically took each unit on and annihilated them. Gaa knew he had moved too fast and had driven himself into this trap and in all probability, they were about to be destroyed to the last man.

Yet, he still threw everything he had at the Hunter. Their only hope was to get a lucky shot that would take the Hunter down and then release them to carry out their prime command for this planet. He committed his air units first and they, each and every one of them, went down in front of the Hunter.

It was like trying to attack a phantom. He was there but when they targeted him it was like he was not there. This golden globe of an object hovering and sliding through the air in one place and then another. Clearly there but not when they got to it, like a will-o-the-wisp.

When he targeted one of the Gilgons it was like a lightning bolt of Zeus smashing into the craft with such power and force there was little but smoke left where the craft had once been. They had committed two hundred thirty-seven of the Gilgons finest crafts and pilots, and in short order two hundred thirty-seven were gone in less time than it took to send them into battle.

Then Hunter turned his attention to the ground units and things really got ugly. When the Hunters weapons struck human and Gilgons alike faced the same fate, total and complete destruction. Their bodies literally coming apart like a rag doll being torn to pieces. No attempt was made to separate human from Gilgon.

The humans had been warned and given the opportunity to evacuate the battle zone and many chose to stay. Some because that was their home and their ingrained need and desire to stay in a familiar place no matter the level of danger or threat to their lives.

The other for the expressed purpose of taking advantage of all those vacant home, offices and businesses left sitting by those who decided to evacuate and come back later to clean up.

No mercy, no concern, no time to consider those who stayed behind. This was a battle between two forces that had one and only one thought in mind, and that was the destruction of the other side. In the end the communities left behind would be leveled and no one, not a single living being or creature would survive the cataclysm that was devouring this place.

From the Superstition Mountains in California and Arizona, the survivors were watching the conflict as it progressed. There was no doubt what they were seeing was something that was clearly from out of this world, and the forces at odds in that place at that time were far beyond anything those of this world could even imagine.

They quickly began to realize that with the battle being controlled and isolated as it was all of the rest of their nation and the world was being spared the conflagration this place was experiencing and for that they were grateful.

The battle progressed as this strange orb dove and rose time and again as it cleansed the land and sky of any and all element of the opposing force. Slowly the firing of weapons from the Gilgons subsided as they were each in their own neutralized and destroyed.

The battle went on for hours and seemed to have no end. It was after the battle had been raging for almost five hours that they noticed the areas of resistance were being reduced and compressed into one location at the southern end of the Salton Sea.

The Hunter had tracked down each element of the Gilgon forces and was now driving them toward the north, toward the sea sitting there at their backs. They were concentrating their forces there for a last stand against the Hunter; a stand that would be useless and short lived. The amount of weapon fire was staggering to those watching as the golden orb moved in closer and closer to the remnants of the Gilgon forces. Its movements were direct, non-stoppable and overpowering.

The end was coming and it was as if one was witnessing the coming of hell itself. As the orb drifted down on the trapped aliens there came a rain of fire and power from the ship that was beyond one's ability to even imagine as powerful and destructive as it was. From the sanctuary of the Superstitions some two hundred fifty miles away the survivors could see the magnitude of the battle unfolding by the Salton. The sky was lit up as if a thousand suns were dancing in the sky over that region illuminating everything.

By the twenties and fifties, they dropped, having their life forces struck from them as efficiently as any precision machine. As each Gilgon fighter died their bodies would then burst into flames and their cremation followed. There was little doubt as to the outcome of this battle and the fact was that outcome was inevitable. As the Gilgons were progressively forced into a tighter pocket Gaa himself was still standing and directing what was left of his force in a final attempt to defeat the Hunter.

The region, which had been sealed by the Hunter, was now only a few hundred yards of area and the standing buildings had been reduced to piles of rubble. The Hunter systematically reduced the remaining force so that Gaa would be the last of the last. He, the Hunter would deal with Gaa one on one and it would not be something Gaa would survive but it would be something that none of his command had or would experience. What was to come was being held just for Gaa and none other.

Finally, the globe dissipated and the Hunter set foot onto the ground in front of Gaa. The two stood there looking at one another. Gaa knew he was facing his executioner but he was not going to back down or bow to this being. No, he would defy him to the bitter end, no matter how he died.

As he thought about it, he preferred to die because of the shame he would face if he returned home. The end result would be his death. No commander returned without his command and Gaa was now without his command. The last of his men had fallen and he was alone.

The entire region from Palm Springs to Phoenix to El Centro to Palm Springs had been laid waste. Not a brick was left standing, not a tree was upright. The entire area had been destroyed to the last inch. There was nothing left. The Gilgons were strewn across this desolate landscape each its own cremation fire. They lay burning and intermingled with the bodies of the humans who had refused to evacuate when they had the chance. The world had never seen such utter and total destruction in any one place in all its history.

The final face down was to take place and the Hunter would complete this competition and send Gaa to oblivion along with his invasion force. Gaa prepared himself as the Hunter raised his arms and swung them in a wide arch and brought his hands down to his side and then pushing his arms with palms facing Gaa forward literally tearing the Gilgon Commander to pieces. It was over and the barrier shield went down and the Hunter reentered his globe and blinked out of sight.

Chapter Fifteen

CALM AFTER THE STORM

Back at the Arizona Superstitions Toni and I had been watching the battle. The level of destruction left us both sick and exhausted. There was a silence over the whole of the mountain range as the tens of thousands that had taken refuge there watched and observed the destruction of everything they had known. The silence was in itself, was deafening and heavy. It was a feeling of defeat. Even knowing the invaders had been destroyed, it was still a loss of monumental proportions.

In addition, they were all, I, Toni and everyone there amazed at the fact that not a single weapon discharge had struck the mountain range. Not a single person or living creature on that mountain range was harmed. Later it would be learned that it was the same at the California Superstitions as well, none had been injured or killed. The ranges had both been protected by a dome of energy or something that simply repulsed any free ranging weapon strikes that were directed at or came at the two mountains ranges.

Whatever the force was over these mountains, it was not penetrable by any weapon fire, and those within it were completely safe. Toni and I stood there watching the others and their reaction to what they had witnessed. It was clear everyone was in a state of bewilderment and shock.

They had witnessed such destruction that they were sure nothing on this earth or off could have survived the battle. The beauty of that place had been reduced to a flat blackened region totally void of anything recognizable. It was clear nothing was salvageable, in fact there was nothing remaining that was even recognizable.

As the sun came over the top of the mountains, we could see out across the land that had once been Phoenix. We all felt and saw the shield dissipate and it was then when everyone started to move down out of the

Superstitions and back into the Phoenix area. No one really knew what they were going to do. All they wanted to do was go back to where their homes had been and see if there was anything that could be recovered.

Toni and I stayed in the car watching the slow migration back to the area that had once been Phoenix. There was nothing to say at the time, it was just too much to comprehend and too much to take in. It had been far greater an event than even they had thought possible.

Not only had every structure in the area been completely destroyed, but the land had been leveled. Wherever there had been a rise it was now gone. Areas that had been lower were now filled in by the debris of the structures that had been knocked down. The terrain had been completely re-structured.

It was maybe four hours later when we felt the presence of the Hunter again. This time he was directing us to a location in the Superstition Mountains. We were told to leave our car and walk due east in the parking area to a trail that went up into a cut in the mountain side. We were to walk a quarter mile till we came to a fork in the trail. At the fork we were to take the left trail and continue until we came to an outcropping. Just around the outcropping we would find an entrance to a cave. We were to enter the cave.

Twenty minutes later Toni and I were entering the cave. At first it seemed quiet but as we stood there and listened, we could hear the humming coming from deeper in the cave. I took the lead and moved on into the cave. As we came to a turn in the tunnel and rounded it, I saw a light ahead of us.

That led us to a chamber. As we approached and entered the chamber, we saw an individual standing at a table with his back to us. First, I, and then Toni stepped into the chamber and stopped and watched the man as he was collecting papers laid out on the table.

As we entered the chamber he stopped and slowly turned, facing us. I recognized him immediately as the truck driver I had worked for back in Black Mountain. Toni knew him from the shooting incident in Miami.

"Welcome, please come in and have a seat over here by the table." The two of us moved across the chamber and sat down. As we were moving to the table the man moved around on the opposite side of the table from where we took our seats.

We sat there looking at each other and then the Hunter spoke. "You have done well in carrying out your obligations to your fellow beings. You also surprised me with the level of intellect and creativity you possessed. You did well and now you can return to your normal lives without any further fear of the Gilgons. Your world is now safe and free of any further threat from them."

I was clearly building up a head of steam and anger as the Hunter spoke. "What the hell do you mean about us doing a good job? Look at the damage and destruction you carried out across this region of the world. You killed thousands of people and completely destroyed that area of California and Arizona. You are a greater danger than those others were, those Gilgons."

The Hunter remained silent and patient and let me vent my anger. I continued to berate the Hunter and blame him for all that had happened to Toni and I over these past months. Finally, I started to calm down and then realized the Hunter was saying or doing nothing other than sitting there listening and letting me vent my anger.

Toni was doing the same and watching the Hunter for any signs of his becoming angry. There were none. He sat there and waited for the storm to come to an end. And so, she did the same. There was little if anything she could do right then. It was a matter of time before I would finally calm down and then we could continue with our meeting with the Hunter.

It was about that time that I began to realize that no one was saying anything in return or making any remarks about what I was saying. I realized I was the only one talking and the other two were sitting there waiting for my tirade to end. I started to calm down and then came to a stop and sat there looking back and forth between the two of them.

The Hunter finally stood up and walked around the table and stood there before the two of us. It was then he started to talk. "Over a million years ago the Gilgons started to venture into the galaxy. They had been invited to become a part of the Universal Council and had rejected that invitation. The Council then tried to isolate them in their original region of the galaxy and that worked for a while. About a thousand years later they started reaching out to other worlds and taking advantage of them.

Their main goal was the location of worlds with resources they needed. When they found them, they would strip those worlds of all their resources and leave them and the native inhabitants virtually destroyed without a possibility of surviving. Many a world went that way until the Universal Council came up with a way of countering their activities. That is when the Hunter came into being.

During these past century's we have carried on a continual battle against the Gilgons never ending attempt to expand to other worlds and victimizing them. At this point, we are successful in the defense of eight out of nine worlds that have been invaded. But that does not mean it has been an easy task for those worlds. They have been damaged severely in the process of gaining their freedom from the Gilgons. This you have experienced.

Could I have dealt with the Gilgons without the amount of damage done? The answer to that is yes, but that would mean, in time, the world and its people would forget what has taken place. The presence of the Gilgons would fade and they would become vulnerable to their coming back and trying again. No, it is best the lesson be taught and taught in a manner in which they will never forget. That is the main defense against the Gilgons.

Next is the location of this action. Could I have dealt with the Gilgons across the whole of this world? The answer to that is yes but there would have been extensive damage across the whole of this planet, and the numbers of people that would die would have been a thousand times more than what happened here. It is clearly better to deal with them in one controlled location.

The people of this region were warned and advised to evacuate, many did and many did not. Those who evacuated have lived and those who stayed have died, it is that simple. They had their choice and they chose to stay and they also paid the price.

The sacrifice of the people at the stadium was something that could not be avoided. There had to be some kind of bait and you were that bait. But it also had to be an area that would be normal for persons of your age and the activity that was taking place.

Next the action had to be of such a magnitude the world would see there was something so dangerous to this world that there was no question of that fact. The world had to witness the magnitude of the forces that are out of this world and a threat to this world. That was done as well.

Last there had to be something that would draw the Gilgons into this region and set them up so they could be completely eliminated. That had to be. You cannot send them off a planet and then expect it to end. They would then come back with three times the numbers and attack with total vengeance. No, they had to be destroyed to the last person and that was done.

He walked around from behind the table again and we both followed him. This world is about to enter into the open space of the galaxy. We will welcome you when that time actually comes, but that will not be until you clear or travel beyond your solar system. What we can give you is relief in the assurance that any future invasion of Gilgons or any other predators will not happen. You are safe from that.

You will learn in time, what the requirements are for membership in the Universal Council. Until then we will oversee your progress and wait for you to achieve that which you must before receiving the invite. It is a violent place out there among the stars and you must be able to accept that and deal with it. Until then you will remain here and protected.

Chapter Sixteen

THE FINAL CHAPTER

Your nation will rebuild in this area even though the immediate area of the battle can never be occupied again. It will be a scar on the face of your planet as a reminder of the fact that you had fought for your life and won your freedom. It will be a memorial to those whose lives were sacrificed for the rest of your world.

As for the two of you, your lives are now joined and you will live them together to your end time. Please live the years to come in peace, and remember this time as a time when the world met the threat and overcame it. You were a significant part of that resistance and you handled it well. For that you will be rewarded.

The Hunter then turned and walked over to a second tunnel leaving the chamber. He entered that tunnel and turned to us and motioned for us to follow him. We got out of our seats, still in a state of total surprise about all he had said. Obviously, there was not going to be any time for questions. He had given us all the answers.

We walked into the tunnel and fell in behind him. He walked us back for about a quarter a mile when we came to a wall and in that wall was a crack about forty-two inches wide. He entered that crack and we continued to follow. About fifty feet into the crack, we came out into another chamber. We found ourselves standing in a place where someone had been hording bags of something.

The Hunter walked over to one of the bags and up ended it on the floor and what came out was something that we would never have expected. We had heard of the Lost Dutchman's mine, but never in our wildest dreams thought that anyone, let alone Toni and I would find it. We just did. Well, the fact was the Hunter found it and was now giving it all to us.

I looked over at Toni and she was standing there trying to grasp what was happening. Her eyes were as big as plates and she was shaking all over. I put my arms around her and held her. The Hunter turned to us. You have both lost everything and have suffered a never-ending threat for months on end. You have earned this and I know that you will use it well.

He then advised that there was a second chamber another thirty feet through that crack and that there were a number of bags in that chamber as well. The first thing that hit me was how we were going to move all that gold out of there and to the banks without being found out. I was sick with the thought of it. The Hunter smiled. "We will move it all together. Now where are you two planning on living the rest of your lives?"

Toni and I looked at each other, "The rest of our lives?" It hadn't sunk in that it would be possible that Toni and I would stay together.

She turned her face toward me and I could see the question in her eyes. She said nothing, just stood there looking at me. Clearly it was my moment and my decision.

"Yes, I would like that, if she feels the same way?"

That small impish smile started to form on her lips and I knew what the answer was going to be. "I could not think of a better end to this story than spending the rest of my life with you Darrel. That is, if you would really have me, as crazy as I can get from time to time."

I felt myself smiling and walked over to her. "That is the exact thing that I love about you the most. There is nothing I do not like about you and right this moment I am asking you if you will marry me as soon as possible?"

Here we go again, the tears started to run as she stood there shaking her head. "God, I have been waiting for this day my whole life. And to think that I would run into my dream in a situation like this is completely unbelievable. But, before you change your mind my answer is yes, a big YES."

As we went through our customary process of formalizing our union the Hunter stood there watching with great interest. Every new culture was intriguing to him and he never passed up the opportunity to witness one of their formal customs. This one he particularly liked.

Finally, we had finished our sealing of the question and the Hunter then interrupted. "Well, that is most interesting, but I'm, afraid we need to get to work and get this stuff moved. So where are you going to want to go to live?"

We both stood there looking at one another. Neither one of us had ever thought about where we really wanted to live, to spend our lives together. Now that the question was being asked, we needed to come up with something.

Hunter was standing there waiting. I looked at Toni and she then stood up on her toes and whispered into my ear the place she wanted to live. I looked at her and knew right then and there it was the perfect place for us.

I looked over at Hunter and he nodded his head and turned toward all the gold, raised his arm and literally moved every bag of gold in the first room into the air. A gold orb formed around the bags and he stepped into the orb, turned toward us and motioned for both of us to enter the orb.

At that point a panel appeared in front of the Hunter and he moved his hands over it and the orb started to move. It literally pushed itself through the crack forcing the mountain open as it went. Once clear of that area it then moved across the cave and out the opening and moved off into the air. It was a little uncomfortable to be standing there looking down and around us as we moved up and away from the ground. It only seemed like seconds and we were decelerating and going down.

We finished the first run and returned to the Superstitions to pick up the rest of the gold. As we left the cave Hunter turned his weapons on the cave and obliterated it. There was nothing left that would give you any idea that a cave had been there, not even a sign of the entrance of the cave remained to be found.

We returned to the place we had unloaded the first load of bags. It was an old smelter that was no longer running. We entered the main furnace building and the Hunter fired up the furnace and then prepared to refine the gold. Don't ask me what he used to fire up the furnace, just know that he did and he then refined the gold into individual bars of twenty-two pounds each. Each bar was branded with our names and the purity of the gold that they were made of. In our case it was .999 gold.

That was just great but what were we going to do with all those gold bars. He smiled at us and then commenced to move all the bars to the Orb and we set out again. The gold was deposited into a gold exchange in our names. How he did that I can't say either, all I know is that he did it and we had our wealth completed.

He stayed with us until we had all the gold deposited and the monies properly received and banked. Clearly, he knew the ways and means of dealing with raw gold and it all went smoothly, something that Toni and I would never have been able to do on our own.

Once that project was completed, he took us to the region where we had decided to live. There we found a motel where he left us. We had no belonging, no car, nothing other than what we were carrying and that included our financial wealth. As he left us, he wished us the best and then was gone.

We had a lot to do including buying some land and building our dream home. But first we needed transportation and the other necessities that people tend to need. We had the money now to do whatever we desired and we desired to build our new life together.

In the mean time we moved into a rental house near the town of Shelton, Washington and started our search for the location and land of our dreams. Our target was Stretch Island located in the Puget Sound on the west side of the Sound just a short distance from Shelton. There was a bridge access between the island and the mainland, a perfect set up for us.

At ten forty-five in the morning on a bright and clear August day a young couple drove into the small town of Shelton, Washington and went to the largest realtor in the area, sat down with an agent and started looking for a rental and land to build on. The newlyweds were excited and eager to start their new life and the agent knew that he was dealing with a couple who could and would be able to pay for whatever it was they wanted or needed.

Over the course of the past two weeks, they had been given a new life and their past experiences had been left behind. The Hunter had seen that all their banking and gold conversion needs had been done and they now had a leading financial adviser on the job overseeing their wealth.

These two had gone through a lot and had seen more than one young couple should have to witness. The time Hunter spent with them was designed to ease those memories. They could not be removed but they could be altered and dulled off and that task he had completed successfully.

Having completed that and then meeting with the leaders of this world cultures, he made it clear the world had successfully come through the attack of the Gilgons and they were now on their way to achieving a successful growth into the outer reaches of the galaxy.

He made it clear as to the obligations they had before being permitted into the greater reaches of space and if they failed to achieve those goals then they would be denied access to all that was out there waiting for them.

There was no doubt left they either conformed to the mandates of the Universal Council or they would never be permitted outside this solar system. Learn to live and work together or live-in isolation from the rest of the galaxy. With the demonstration of the power and weaponry of the Hunter and the absolute requirements for access to the rest of the galaxy there was little doubt the Hunter was serious and they, the Universal Council, had the ability and power to enforce their mandates.

It was six months later and Toni and I were sitting at a table in our favorite restaurant during lunch, when I saw the stranger enter the place and start looking around. He finally zeroed in on us and started walking toward us. He was a big man and his head never held still for a second as he walked through the tables toward us.

It was then that I noticed his hand and the three fingers on them and I braced for what was coming. I reached over to Toni and took her hand. "Hon, they've found us."

She turned her head toward the man and watched him walking toward us. I couldn't believe it, there was a Gilgon right there in the restaurant and walking right at us. Both his hands were clearly empty and no weapon was visible. How could the Hunter have missed even one? He was just too thorough to have done that and so I started to think that maybe this being was not bad news, we would know shortly.

He walked up and without being invited sat down in a chair across from me. He sat there looking at the two of us and I can assure you he was seeing two totally surprised and scared individuals; the air was charged with emotions as he sat down.

The three of us sat there looking at one another, Toni and I waiting for the stranger to say something. Finally, he placed both hands down on the table top and leaned toward them. "My name is Qee and I am here to take care of loose ends. You two were directly involved in the failure of Gaa and his unit in the overcoming of this world and for that we still owe you."

I sat there looking at him and remembering what the Hunter had told me about the Gilgons, though their appearance was intimidating their strength was less than that of a small woman on this planet. It took everything they had to function under the gravitational pull of our planet and that gave the men of this planet the upper hand. I was watching him and preparing myself for a short period of exertion while dealing with this being.

He continued. "Unless the two of you want this entire village totally destroyed you will get out of your chairs and walk ahead of me out of this place. There is a van parked out front and you will enter that van and sit in the back seat and remain quiet. One false move and we will hit this village with everything we have. It's all up to you."

He waited for my response. I reached over and took Toni's hand and stood up and started to move for the front door. As we approached the door, I saw the van and the two other men sitting in it. I knew that if we got into that van, we had no chance of surviving. Yet I also had to think of the people of this town and their future.

As we approached the front door I reached out and turned the latch locking the door and turned facing this Qee. "You are not going to do anything to this town nor are you taking Toni and me anywhere."

That stopped him short and he stood there looking at me. He started to pull his jacket open and I reached out and took hold of his arm and squeezed until he was starting to lean in the direction of my hand. The pained look in his face was obvious and I felt him relax. "I could kill you in an instant, but right now I choose to let you live. Right now, I want you to look across the street to the building directly across from us.

"Look up at the roof and you will see the top of a gold orb just over the rooftop. If you spend a few seconds thinking about it you will recognize that orb as that of the Hunter. Now you have two choices. One you go out to the van get in it and leave and return to you ship and leave this solar system. The other is that you can fight here and now and the Hunter will kill you, your ship, and any other ships that may have accompanied you. None of you will leave here alive.

"Now the choice is yours, so make it now, or die right here and now." I released the grip on his arm and he shook it and then backed away from us and turned so we could go by him. He unlocked the door and walked out to the van and got in. After several minutes, I'm sure they used to communicate with their commander, they drove away.

I looked up and saw the Hunters orb move off down the other side of the building in the same direction the Gilgons had driven. Toni and I returned to our table and sat down to wait. "Darrel, why don't we go home and pack up now and go someplace else?"

I smiled at her. "No, that won't be necessary. Hunter will be here in a few minutes and we will know where we stand and what to expect in the future. Just relax as best as you can and we will wait."

It was thirty minutes later when the door opened and Hunter came walking in. He walked back to our table and sat down and started to shake his head. "They seem to be getting bolder every year. I can assure you those beings will never threaten you again. Their ships were taken care of and their governing body has been informed if any Gilgon ships enter this region of the galaxy it would be total and complete war between them and the Universal Council and its member governing bodies. Enough is enough and any future encroachment in this region will result in total war. They agreed."

We were still a little shaken from the experience but I knew that Hunter had in fact taken care of the issues. "Then it's all right for Toni and me to stay here and build our new lives?"

Before I had finished the question, he was nodding his head yes. "I can assure you that you are no longer under any threat from the Gilgons. They took one step too many and have now worked themselves into a potential war with eighty percent of the advanced technologies in the galaxy. You and this world will never hear from them again. That warning from the Council is as much as a death sentence and they know it."

So, there you have it. I really don't know what else I can say at this time. I lost my two best friends when this thing, this adventure started and I will never ever forget them. I was lucky. In fact, I was lucky in several ways. I lived, I found my life's love, and I survived it all.

I guess the lesson learned from this whole thing was that there are forces out there in the Universe that are not friendly. They are in fact predatory in nature and a direct threat to any world that is developing an advanced intelligence. It would behoove us of this world to remember this time and event for what it actually was, a lesson on the habits and threats of those visiting our world, whatever their reason or purpose.